The Summer
Sherman
Loved
Me

The Summer Sherman Loved Me

Jane St. Anthony

FARRAR STRAUS GIROUX / NEW YORK

www.fsgkidsbooks.com

Library of Congress Cataloging-in-Publication Data
St. Anthony, Jane.
    The summer Sherman loved me / Jane St. Anthony.— 1st ed.
        p.   cm.
    Summary: In addition to coping with her changing relationship with
her mother, twelve-year-old Margaret spends her summer trying to sort
out her feelings for the boy next door who claims to love her.
    ISBN-13: 978-0-374-37289-7
    ISBN-10: 0-374-37289-6
    [1. Interpersonal relations—Fiction.   2. Mothers and daughters—
Fiction.   3. Family life—Fiction.]   I. Title.

PZ7.S1413Sum 2006
[Fic]—dc22
                                                        2005046361

for Louis
who *led* me to Kate
who *led* me to Jane Resh Thomas

The Summer
Sherman
Loved
Me

"Margaret, I love you," Sherman Jenson whispered loudly from his porch across our front yards the first time I slept on my porch during summer vacation.

I lay still. My face and body were lower than the windowsill. From next door, Sherman must have seen me come out. My chest swelled with pressure. My heart was too full.

A dull thud followed from next door, then the muffled cries of Bobby, Sherman's brother. Sherman was older and larger than Bobby. Bobby's legs were so skinny there didn't seem to be room for bones in them.

"Margaret?"

Suddenly Sherman's voice was so close to my ear that it seemed to be in my head. He had come outside. His face pressed against the porch screen.

"Margaret?"

Was I supposed to say something? Was this supposed to be a conversation?

"Margaret," Sherman said, "come outside."

When we were younger, Sherman and I rode bikes together in the summer. He liked to show off for me, riding with no hands. I hardly ever saw him up close anymore.

Sherman Jenson was almost thirteen. He had the kind of arms that could rescue girls. His voice had dropped so that he sounded more like his dad than his mom when he yelled at Bobby. He was blond. He was cute. And I—too tall, with brown hair and no memorable features—must look cute to him, if he loved me.

But leave the porch? It was already halfway outside. In our family we never unlocked the doors at night except in an emergency, such as when one grandparent fell and the other one called us to come over and help. The sliding bolt on the porch door was our only protection against the unknown.

And now Sherman had invited me out. A date, almost. How could I not go? I hugged my bare arms, wanting to be covered by more than a thin nightgown.

"Just a minute," I whispered back to Sherman. As soon as I spoke, I wished I had pretended to be asleep.

One of the twins had abandoned her baby doll on a lawn chair on the porch. The doll lay wrapped in a piece of old doll blanket secured at her neck. I undid the safety pin and threw the blanket around my shoulders, fastening the pin over the lump in my throat. Then I walked to the door and slid the bolt out of its bracket as quietly as I could.

Sherman sat on the lawn between our houses. I walked to-

"Boys and girls don't mix in the dark," Mother told my brother, Mark, and me when we wanted to sleep on the porch at the same time. Mark was nine, three years younger. Neither of us knew exactly what Mother meant. So we took turns: my night, his night. At three and a half, the twins were too young for a turn.

But here I was in the dark, speeding into more dark, with a boy. I blinked away Mother's disapproving face.

By moonlight the park occupied a different planet, earth-like but with a crackly atmosphere. Sherman biked ahead of me, over the grass and down the wide path between the tennis courts and the ball field. The playground equipment was deserted. A breeze pushed the swings slightly, as if someone had jumped off just a minute ago. Maybe at night, ghost children played on the swings and teeter-totter and slide.

Sherman continued along the paved stretch. As I tried not to think about ghosts, Sherman paused at the water fountain.

"Where are we going?" I asked, looking at the side of his face, not his bare chest.

"I don't know," he said, scanning the far end of the park as if he expected to see something new. "Let's ride the thirteen bumps."

I would rather sit on a swing next to children's spirits than ride Bobby's bike, or anyone's bike, down the thirteen bumps.

The bumps were rises on a long sloping hill behind the mansion at the edge of the park property. When I was nine, Sherman and Roger Colby and other neighborhood kids leaned over the deep basement window and peered into the vine-covered old house, where they saw a witch, so they said. They screamed and ran backward, some of them stumbling. They told me to look. I was sure my heart would stop when the witch locked her eyes with mine.

Instead I saw three men in suits who stood talking next to a rolltop desk. Even though I saw the men, I still believed that the witch lived there. Maybe the men had been sent to kill her. Or perhaps she had trapped them. I couldn't say anything to Sherman and Roger and the others. I walked back to the playground without seeing them. I had frozen inside.

Now Sherman stood close to that house, his bare feet in grass that was colorless in the dark. He held his bike at his side as if it were a horse. "I'll go first," he said.

Was this a competition?

Once again behind the witch's house, I couldn't speak. I had

When I woke up in the morning, the twins' voices were a stream of sound from the backyard. I hid under the sheet.

Last night needed a better ending. On the porch, I had been part of the night with its own soft breath. Then Sherman had entered and, with him, the promise of something exciting. But why didn't he touch my hand or act as if he wanted to hold it? Did he wreck everything on purpose or accidentally? Was it all over now?

I walked into the house and through the living room and dining room to the bedroom that I shared with the twins when it wasn't my turn to sleep on the porch. Our room was the largest of three bedrooms. Dad had divided it with a wall of tall bookcases that he had built with shelves on both sides. I always knew when the twins were on their side, but I wouldn't be able to see them unless they grew almost to the ceiling.

After I dressed, I went into the kitchen. Even though I dreaded what Kathleen might have said to Mother, I was too hungry to stay away. This was only the second morning in my life that I had been allowed to have a sugar cereal, if Mark hadn't finished it. I had begged Mother before she did her weekly shopping. For once, she had given in.

I poured the sugarcoated flakes. A waterfall of black ants fell through the air. Each ant looked as if it were trying to grab on to a sugary flake for a parachute as it fell. I dropped the box. My scream stayed in my throat. I wouldn't let it out. If Mother saw this, she would never buy another sugar cereal again. Hurriedly, I emptied my bowl into the garbage and pushed the cereal box on top.

"What are you doing?" asked Mother, appearing suddenly in the basement doorway with her laundry basket. Her forehead was damp, and dark circles pooled under her eyes. She did a lot of housework but she never seemed as excited about it as other moms did. She didn't make toaster covers for fun.

"I'm taking the garbage out," I said, crumpling the top of the garbage bag, hoping the ants wouldn't decide to break out. "It's full."

Mother stared. Had I ever taken the garbage out voluntarily? She and her laundry basket went out the door into the backyard.

On my return from the garbage can behind the garage, I stopped to sit on the sandbox bench. The twins glanced at me while their hands stayed busy in the sand.

"Sherman is my cross to bear," Mrs. Jenson told my mother

as she rested her laundry basket on our shared fence. The bobby pins in her pin curls caught the sun's light. She didn't usually bother tying a scarf over her little twists of hair.

Mrs. Jenson reminded my mother often about her crosses. Gary, the Jenson teenager, and Bobby were crosses to bear, too.

"Joan, Sherman is a good boy," said Mother.

Mother kept one ear aimed at Mrs. Jenson while she fitted the legs of my brother's good slacks over the metal frames that stretched out the wrinkles. She would still have to iron them, but less.

"One girl," Mrs. Jenson said. "If only I had just one little girl."

I piled up sand as fast as I could before Kathleen whacked it with her little plastic shovel. Mrs. Jenson would have matching girls if I were in charge.

"Sherman put sewing needles in the couch cushions this morning," said Mrs. Jenson to Mother. "He did that so Bobby would sit on them when he came down to watch cartoons."

Mrs. Jenson had bought a new couch the first year she was married. According to her plan, she would buy one every ten years. Pinholes and other couch catastrophes threatened to throw the math off. We rarely sat on our own couch, so it would probably last through infinity. You stuck to the clear plastic cover in the summer. In the winter, the cover was cold and stiff.

Next door, Sherman sat in the Jensons' lone surviving apple tree. He pelted Bobby with dirty old tennis balls. Bobby screamed a long, sky-scratching wail.

Love surrounded me. In books. On the radio. In movies. If Sherman really loved me, why was he in his yard tormenting his brother? Why had he tormented me with his stupidity?

In the sandbox, Kathleen refused to let Karen have a turn with the shovel.

"Get one of the shovels that's in the grass," I said. "Or use the spoon."

Their four hands fought for the shovel as if it were the Holy Grail. I grabbed Kathleen's wrist, forcing her to release the attack toy. She tried to sink her teeth into my thigh, but I easily held her back with my hand. Kathleen shrieked and lunged at Karen, who made a show of innocence. I wrapped my arm around Kathleen's waist and hung on so that Karen could play by herself for a few minutes.

Mother turned to look at us. Her eyes begged: Please, just give me time to get the wash up.

Mrs. Jenson slowly turned away from the fence and walked to her clothesline. She hung up Mr. Jenson's sleeveless under-shirts and boxers, one clothespin at a time biting into the fabric. Up and down. Clean to dirty to clean. Over and over, Mrs. Jenson and my mother in a procession of tasks that never ended.

I pictured myself hanging out Sherman's clothes: the white

T-shirts with front pockets and his cutoffs that would flutter in the warm breeze.

Mrs. Jenson started on the boys' briefs, sloppily now, only one clothespin per pair.

Bobby ran into the house. The screen door slammed. Sherman's backside descended the tree, his legs gripping it expertly. He raced up the steps and inside. I couldn't see his face, only the back of his smooth head. Sherman was a golden crew cut on a body full of heat and light. The screen door slammed again. Bobby started shrieking.

At ten o'clock in the morning, the sun streamed through the gaps in the elm tree branches over the sandbox.

"Put your hands down flat, this way," I told the twins.

At first they put their palms up. I turned their hands over and piled bucketfuls of sand onto them. They wriggled their fingers upward and screamed with happiness. Mother paused to look at them. Her hands lingered on the clothesline, holding the straps of a pink sunsuit with little white lambs on it.

"That's how you looked when you were their age," she said to me. "So darling."

I imagined what she didn't say: So darling. But why have you grown away from me?

The Jensons' back door slammed again. Sherman bolted. I flushed with confusion as he raced out of the yard.

"Will you watch the girls now?" Mother asked.

I stood in the kitchen, checking for ants in the cereal cupboard. I turned to look at Mother, empty laundry basket at her side.

"I'm taking the casserole to church for Mrs. Albright's funeral," she said.

If Kathleen and Karen walked the eight blocks to church with her, she would be gone for about a month. On a good day, I would have reminded her that they were her twins, not mine.

"Okay," I said, fearing any more words that might slip out of her. "Fine."

"Thank you for letting Kathleen sleep on the porch with you," Mother said. "She's been fussy at night lately."

She stared hard at me. I couldn't decide whether it was a regular stare or a stare meant to drag a confession out of me. Sometimes they blurred. Besides, wouldn't she have confronted me by now if Kathleen had blabbed? Mother's laundry basket drooped at her side, resting on her leg. During the day she wore nylons, even in the summer, but the old ones with runs and snags.

"I'm going to the library with Grace this afternoon," I said. We went to the lake only as often as we could get away. But our weekly trip to the library was set in stone. "That's after you get back."

She moved across the kitchen to the basement door and went through as if someone only she could hear had called to her from downstairs.

After she left for church in her evening nylons, I made peanut-butter-and-banana sandwiches for the girls' lunch and myself, as I hadn't had breakfast. Mark came into the kitchen and demanded food. I had an extra sandwich ready, knowing that he always showed up when food appeared.

"Take everything outside," I told him. "Eat at the picnic table so I don't have to clean up your mess."

Mark looked insulted, being the second oldest. "I'm not a slob like them," he said.

"Then stop stuffing watermelon into the squirt guns," I said. "It just messes them up, and besides, it doesn't work."

"I don't want to eat with you anyway," Mark said. "You and your babies." His hand darted into the refrigerator and emerged with a ring of bologna.

"That has to last all week," I snapped at him.

"Who are you?" he said. "Mom?"

He stomped out with the bologna and a butter knife. In general I didn't dislike him, but I was happy to have him gone. If Kathleen talked about last night, I didn't want anyone around.

"More bananas in my sandwich?" Kathleen asked.

A tree full of them, I thought as I sliced another banana. Kathleen opened her sandwich as if it were a book. She was dangerous, too young to be successfully bribed. The twins took a few banana slices out of their sandwiches and tried to spear them with their chubby fingers. The soft slices broke every time.

"Try a straw," I said. They looked at me with wonder. I slid a piece of banana onto the end of a straw and added another, then another. The girls beamed as if I had made a dancing poodle appear.

By the time I had cleaned up the mess, Mother was back, looking even more damp.

"I have to go meet Grace," I said, grabbing my books and heading for the door.

"You could at least say goodbye," Mother said.

"It *is* good to get away," I said, knowing how the words would bruise her. "Bye."

Why couldn't she be the mother I deserved: cooler and looser? She loved having me in her lap when I was a twin-size person. I would spill everything in my head into her ears. Now I imagined her X-ray vision probing my brain for signs of rebellion. My bike ride with Sherman violated sacred rules: No leaving the house without telling where you were going. No leaving the porch when you slept on it. No boy-girl stuff. And no dead neighbor boy due to any of the above.

Out of the house, I switched from worrying about Mother to worrying about how to avoid Sherman. In the garage, I put the library books in the bike basket and wheeled my bike out and through the gate, trying to be as small and quiet as possible.

Inching my bike across the driveway, I looked toward Sherman's garage. No signs of life there. I pedaled in the opposite direction, slowly. Even the movement of air might remind Sherman of my presence in the world. I didn't want that right now.

Grace waited for me on her corner, which was on my route to the library. "We're free!" she called.

Grace rode her bike with one hand lightly touching the handlebars as if the bike steered itself and she was just along for the ride. I told her what had happened at the park with Sherman.

"You mean you had to run down the hill to see that he wasn't dead?" she asked. "He wanted you to think he was *dead*, in the *park*, at *night*?" Her mouth tightened with disgust. She gripped her handlebars with both hands. "What a jerk," she continued, shaking her head as if she wanted to loosen it from her shoulders.

Her anger made me stronger. Grace, my best friend, a crusader, felt injustice deeply. Her happy freckles seemed to dance across her nose when she took on a cause.

The library was a good place to not think about Sherman. He probably couldn't even picture the inside of one. Grace chose her books with certainty. I moved slowly, examining titles. If I survived a nuclear war and the library didn't, the books I chose had better be good ones.

Miss Tate, the librarian, smiled at me with a knowing look when we checked our books out. She treated me as though we had a secret, which we did.

"Your middle name?" she had asked when I applied for a library card with the first-grade class.

"Beatrice," I told her, rolling my eyes quickly to show her it wasn't my idea.

"You like your middle name as much as I used to like my first name," she said.

Later, when I learned to read better, I saw that her nameplate said Beatrice Tate. I appreciated that she had given me a lot of winks even before I understood the joke.

Grace usually came over to my house to read after we went to the library. Her house was a zoo, even without twins. Once home, we parked our bikes in the backyard. The twins splashed in the wading pool. Mother unpinned the clothes from the line.

Mark was making Kool-Aid in the kitchen. "Sherman brought that over for you," he said, pointing with the wooden spoon to a grocery bag under the kitchen table. Drops of purple liquid fell from the spoon to the floor.

"Did Mother see it?" I asked him.

"No. She was in the basement when Sherman came."

"Better not let her in on this," Grace said.

I picked up the bag and went out to the porch, Grace right with me.

"Open it," she said.

I sat on a lawn chair with the bag in my lap. It was so light that it felt empty. The top was crumpled shut. I opened it, put my hand inside, and felt around with my fingertips.

"Ow!" I cried, but not so loudly that Mother would hear. Something had pricked my finger.

"Tip it out, whatever it is," said Grace.

A rose fell into my lap. It was scarlet, and the petals were so velvety that I touched them to my cheek. Then I pushed my nose into its center and took such deep breaths that I wondered if I would use up all the perfume. A thin white satin ribbon made a bow around the thorny stem.

"Shake the bag again," Grace said, as though she had X-ray vision and knew there was more inside.

I shook it. A little envelope fell out. My name was on the front, in handwriting that made me embarrassed to know a person who wrote so badly.

"Open it," said Grace.

I pulled the card out. It was flat, not the open-up kind, with little blue violets growing around the edges.

" 'Forgiv me,' " Grace read over my shoulder. " 'I love you.' "

"Maybe it's an apology for being an idiot," she commented.

"He doesn't know that 'forgive' has an 'e,' " I said.

"What are you going to do with the rose?" Grace asked. "Give it back?"

Where would Sherman find a perfect rose, a white ribbon that wasn't from Christmas, and an unused card with blue violets?

"What are you going to do?" Grace asked again.

"I don't know," I said. "You know my mom thinks boyfriends shouldn't happen until you're about fifty. So I have to hide it from her."

Or I could just think about Sherman.

"What are you doing?" Karen asked, staring into my half of the bedroom as I stuffed the rose under my mattress. I couldn't put the rose in water in a jelly glass as Mother did with the dandelions that the twins picked for her. The rose linked me to Sherman in a way Mother wouldn't like.

"Tucking my sheets in," I said in a mean voice. But I didn't feel safe. When Karen left, I placed the slightly flattened rose very carefully in my cardboard box of treasures. The beautiful fragrance wafted upward as I shut the top and replaced the box under my bed.

Sherman disappeared, at least from my sight, for a few days. I imagined that he had turned into the rose. When I was older, maybe sixteen or seventeen, I could put him in water, and he would revive. Then he would be a normal person who knew how to spell and had better ideas about dates. If I ran into him, what would I say to him about love, the rose, and his stupid stunt at the park?

Finally, after nearly a week of no Sherman, I saw Bobby at the side of the Jensons' house. He was spraying himself with the hose to cool off.

I mustered up my courage to ask the burning question. I knew I could relax if Sherman had gone to his grandparents' house or was helping his father, an electrician. He did that sometimes when his mother needed to not see him for a while.

"Where has Sherman been?" I asked Bobby through the porch window.

"He's working with Dad up north," said Bobby, turning with the hose, so that he sprayed me through the screen. "Mom's mad at Sherman because she saw Mr. Underwood at the butcher shop, and he said somebody clipped a couple of his roses."

My body felt sick, as if it were going to throw up through its pores. "Why does she think Sherman did it?" I asked.

Bobby held the hose behind him, so that the spray arched onto his own porch. "She always thinks it's Sherman when something bad happens," he said.

"Oh," I answered. My tongue didn't seem to work anymore.

"Gotta go," said Bobby. He walked away with the spray pounding on his neck.

Had Sherman stolen the rose from Mr. Underwood? He

worked with Mr. Underwood sometimes, mowing the lawn or edging the sidewalk. They talked a lot in the backyard. With only one house in between ours and the Underwoods', I had a clear view of who was over there. The Underwoods' backyard looked like a magazine photo compared to Sherman's half-bald yard strewn with car parts and old bats and balls.

My brain swam around inside my head looking for answers. Nothing.

Mark walked onto the porch. He looked surprised to see me standing there. "What are you doing?" he said.

"I'm thinking."

"Oh. About what?"

I had no privacy. He wanted the contents of my head. "Nothing. Bobby is looking for you."

Mark's face lit up. He lost interest in me and left.

My brain resumed its work. I had to talk to Mr. Underwood, although I couldn't imagine what I would say. He was old, but his mother was older. She always stopped to talk to kids when she was out for a slow walk with her cane. Mr. Underwood was friendly, too. All the parents laughed a lot when he was around.

Now that he was retired, Mr. Underwood spent even more time in his garden, sometimes with his shirt off. No kids want to see dads or other men without a shirt. Some men had hair on their backs, as if spots of chest hair weren't awful enough. Mr. Underwood wasn't very hairy, but it didn't matter.

I suddenly realized that the twins might be useful. Mother

could see me if I went over to the Underwoods'. I needed a reason to be in their perfect yard.

"I'm taking the twins out later," I told Mother during the twins' nap time. "Mr. Underwood would love it if I brought them over to look at his flowers." It wasn't a big lie, as I was certain that Mr. Underwood liked visitors.

Kathleen and Karen were quiet in their half of the bedroom while Mother pretended that they were resting and not playing with their tea set or whatever they did for their nap hour.

Mother stared at me as if she could see the deception. She just couldn't piece it together. "Flowers?" she said. "Why does Mr. Underwood want the twins to see his flowers?"

"Got me," I said, surprised by what was running out of my mouth. "Maybe he wants to chop them up for fertilizer."

Mother looked as if she would start crying, something that she did when my bad side leaked out.

"Just kidding," I said. "You know I'm kidding. I'm sorry."

"They're ready to get up now," she said, patting her eyes with a handkerchief that you could almost see through. "You can take the girls if you want to. But I don't know what's going on."

I wasn't sure either.

The twins had been busy during their nap time. They had exchanged shorts so that each girl wore a mismatched outfit. Kathleen sported yellow sailboats on her shorts and lime-green suckers on her shirt. Karen reversed the pattern with green-sucker shorts topped with yellow boats. They looked as if they had been sawed in half and pasted back together the wrong way.

"We're going to see some flowers," I told them. They looked at me with interest.

"We're going to pick flowers for Mommy," Karen said to Kathleen, translating my words into something more meaningful.

"No, we're going to look at Mr. Underwood's flowers," I said. "No picking, just looking."

When I rang the Underwoods' doorbell, I prayed that no one would answer, especially not Mr. Underwood without a shirt.

"Look who's here, Mother," Mr. Underwood called back into the house when he opened the door to the three of us. He wore a short-sleeved white shirt. "It's the young lady who enjoys nighttime bike rides, and her sidekicks.

"Margaret, my mother will be overjoyed," he said more quietly to me as I walked into the living room.

"Don't make them wait outside in that heat all day, Charles," Mrs. Underwood called from an invisible place. "Invite them in for lemonade."

Before the twins crashed into our lives, Mother and Mark and I used to visit Mrs. Underwood once in a while. We brought the twins a few times, but when they started walking they became windup toys that quickly moved out of sight. The wound-up twins were hard to control amid the Underwoods' breakables, and our visits ceased.

The house was cool, with fans humming in the living room and dining room. We walked through to the kitchen. Everything seemed fragile: slim curved legs on the furniture, china animals on little tables, tiny colored vases that light poured through on a windowsill.

"What a delight it is to have you call on us," Mrs. Underwood said as she served lemonade chilled in the refrigerator. The glass pitcher looked heavy, but Mr. Underwood let his mother handle it.

The twins drank out of real glasses at the table, tripping over themselves as they answered Mrs. Underwood's questions about their age and what they liked to do in the summer.

Mr. Underwood stood in front of the flower-cart wallpaper with his arms folded, as if watching a funny play.

"What motivated you to share your company with us today?" he asked. "I don't believe that you are in the habit of making regular social calls on your elders."

"Oh, we just felt like getting out," I said. "And we wanted to look at your flowers."

"That can be arranged," said Mr. Underwood. "Mother, these young ladies are now going to experience the 'highlights tour,' due to the warmth of the afternoon, and their ages," he added, his eyes resting on the twins.

"You be sure to bring them in to say goodbye before they leave," Mrs. Underwood said. "I don't know when I've had such nice company." She beamed at the twins as if they were big banana splits. "It reminds me of how I enjoyed the visits with you and your mother and brother, Margaret," she said, probably so I wouldn't think she preferred the twins. "She'll have to come again, too."

Kathleen and Karen ran around sticking their noses in the roses outside. Mr. Underwood showed them how to clasp their hands behind their backs so that they wouldn't forget and grab the thorny stems. More kinds of roses than I could have imagined in one yard lived there.

"Each has its own special beauty, almost a personality," Mr. Underwood said as we stood in front of the Charlotte Armstrongs, a popular red rose.

Easily sidetracked, the twins tried to balance on their tiptoes and wash their hands in the birdbath. Based on a lifetime's warnings against touching dead birds, I didn't think that a birdbath was a sanitary basin. Who knew what went on in there? I pulled the twins away.

"Have I seen all the roses?" I asked when we finished our tour. There was one kind of rose Mr. Underwood didn't have: a scarlet one.

"All that I have had the privilege of nurturing," he said. "I do try to introduce a new variety into the family every year or so."

I swallowed hard and said, "Some people think that somebody stole a rose of yours."

"Someone did. Old Man Harding down the block fished around in my garden for an anniversary gift for his wife," Mr. Underwood said. "He is without a doubt the cheapest old coot who ever lived. I raised the alarm. Then I saw the stems on his back steps where he had trimmed them."

No matter how bad his ideas were, at least Sherman hadn't stolen my rose from Mr. Underwood. I pictured him at the florist's two blocks away, putting his bad penmanship on the little card.

We entered the kitchen through the back door. Voices drifted to us from the front of the house. Mr. Underwood, the twins, and I moved through the house, back to front.

"Charles, Sherman came to tell us that he has done no wrong to your garden," Mrs. Underwood said to her son. "He feels unjustly accused by his mother, who saw him with a rose."

Sherman stood in the entryway, a furrow between his eyebrows.

"He is innocent of mischief in our yard," said Mr. Underwood, looking very powerful in his living room, surrounded by short people. "But I can't say what he's been up to at night when the rest of the neighbors are safe in their beds."

Sherman stared at Mr. Underwood without speaking.

I took each twin by one of their hands, which were wet. "Thank you for the lemonade and the tour," I said as I hurried to the front door.

"Come again, girls," said Mrs. Underwood.

Sherman stepped back to let me pass. His hands were cupped together in front of his chest. Something seemed to stir in them. The heat from Sherman's body met me as I brushed past.

Being in love, or figuring out whether to be in love or not, made me tired. I slept later and later in the morning. Summer kept happening.

"Dog days are coming," Mother said, as the Fourth of July neared. "Get all your swimming in now if you want to swim."

The Fourth of July was the cutoff for her. You could swim in a city lake on that day and even that evening. But on July fifth, Mother's face pinched with displeasure if you wanted to go in the water. She made dog days sound as if they were a polio epidemic.

"What are dog days?" I asked her when I was little. "Are they bad?"

"The dogs take over," she told me. "The water isn't safe."

I pictured packs of dogs—big, snarly ones; a canine club of synchronized swimmers, fanning out in formations. They would make a sweep of the lake, scaring to death little kids whose parents didn't know about dog days.

July and August were the hot months when you needed to be in the water. But by then your only choice was a kiddie pool in the backyard.

"Margaret, we're going swimming today," Grace said on the phone. "We have to store it up before dog days."

"We could go downtown for a change," I said. "To a movie. And Bridgeman's."

"We *have* to load up on the lake," Grace stated. "We only get one chance a year."

After four years of Red Cross swimming lessons, I could stay on top of the water only by doing the dog paddle. Grace always dog-paddled out to the raft with me, although she could swim the regular way.

"May I go to the lake with Grace later?" I asked Mother, whose hair was pulled into a knot at the back of her head. Her exposed damp neck made me feel hotter.

"If you've finished the vacuuming," she said. Vacuuming was part of the sacred Saturday morning cleaning ritual. Every Sunday we ate dinner in the dining room. You could count on the twins to drop scalloped corn or green Jell-O with pears onto the carpet. But we had to clean before that happened.

"Remember, no more swimming after the Fourth," she said. I nodded and backed toward the broom closet where the vacuum lived. Did she make this stuff up to torture me?

"Right," I said. "The Fourth. Dogs win."

She looked puzzled, as if not sure whether this was disrespectful or observant. She sighed, and continued dusting with Mark's old underwear.

After I had vacuumed, and dressed again with my bathing suit under my shorts and blouse, I wheeled my bike out of the garage and into the front yard. Grace would meet me at the usual corner.

I biked slowly, barely moving through the humid, sticky air.

"It's going to be a doozy, Margaret," called Mr. Underwood. He straightened up from watering a white rosebush, one of two that puffed out on either side of his front steps. I braked and paused. After he had been so nice to the twins and me, I owed him a little more attention than usual.

"Yes," I said, guessing that was the right response. "The kids already look as if they've been cooked."

"You do have an earnest digger on your premises," said Mr. Underwood.

Mark's shiny face had looked up at me as I left the backyard. He was working on the hole that would lead him to China.

"I plan to spend the afternoon inside with the shades down and the Arctic Ocean in my glass," Mr. Underwood said. "Preserve yourself, Margaret. Mother is looking forward to visiting with you and the little tornadoes again soon."

Mrs. Underwood must have been Mr. Underwood's mother when he was a boy. But I couldn't picture her eyes filling with

Suddenly fingers dug into my upper arms, pulling. When my head surfaced, I felt as if I had broken through a crust. I came out sputtering and sobbing. Grace's voice was alongside me. She must have been paddling with one arm and holding on to me with the other.

"You're okay, Margaret," she said. "You're okay."

The body on my other side moved with me, too, and voices rose out of the splashing around us. Only a few yards separated me from a sandy bottom that my feet could touch. The next thing I knew, I was kneeling on the ground, gasping. My hair stuck to my face, and for a second I wasn't sure where the back of my head was.

A little girl said, "What's wrong with that lady?"

I squinted through my hair and saw knees held up by legs in a semicircle in front of me. I looked up. Between strands of hair, I saw a chest with a whistle hanging on it. Sherman's face was next to the lifeguard's chest. His expression was grim.

Grace came into view. "You're breathing," she said. "That's good. You're okay now."

I tried to look at her. Her forehead was furrowed. She leaned in and dabbed at the side of my mouth with a beach towel. Grace's mouth started moving again while I stared at her furrow. It had a tiny pimple.

"Some stupid idiot thinks he's funny," Grace said. "He pulled you down. Sherman was on the raft. We jumped in and gave you the life buoy."

My hands must have held it, but they didn't seem to remember.

One side of my face sank into the sand. Then my arms, my stomach, my legs felt the heat. My body shook. I wanted it to stop so I could kiss the sand, even though it might get in my mouth. But my head was too heavy to lift and turn.

mother was kind enough to leave the door unlatched so that we might enter, if you'll permit us."

The sight of Sherman and Mr. Underwood unnerved me. "Sure," I said, pulling the sheet up to my chin. I could imagine Mr. Underwood bringing me a Get Well card. But with Sherman?

Mr. Underwood walked across the porch and sat in the lawn chair next to the bed. Sherman placed himself in the red wagon very carefully so that it wouldn't start rolling.

"How are we feeling today?" asked Mr. Underwood, smiling as if we had survived an unexpected adventure together.

"Better," I said. I didn't feel anything except for surprise that the two of them were on the porch. "Normal, I think."

"I am here because Mr. Jenson came to me with a dilemma last night," said Mr. Underwood, nodding at Sherman. I wondered whether Sherman knew what a dilemma was. "I'm very pleased that he consulted me on a matter of moral disquietude. He has the conscience and the integrity to engage a man he believes has the experience to guide him. While my knowledge of the world is limited to the quiet corner I occupy, I daresay that I have tried throughout my life to acquire a broad understanding of how humans conduct—and ought to conduct—themselves in society. I am honored that Mr. Jenson sought me out to assist him in his quest."

Mr. Underwood's words were punctuated by the backfiring of the large Oldsmobile in front of Sherman's house. His

Mother had me rest on the porch bed. "You stay here as long as you want, and I'll bring your supper on a tray," she said.

When she was kind, I was almost more nervous than when she tried to see into my devious self. I decided to reward her by being a better person someday.

Grace hadn't left since Dad had picked us and our bikes up in the station wagon. She sat next to me on a lawn chair, reading my library copy of *A Tree Grows in Brooklyn*.

Mrs. Jenson made doughnuts and sent Bobby over with them.

"Great idea," Grace said. "It can't be more than a hundred and ten degrees outside."

Kathleen and Karen were ordered to stay off the porch. So they leaned over the windowsill between the porch and the living room, rocking on their stomachs.

"Daddy's station wagon is full of sand," Kathleen said in her whisper-scream.

"Margaret was full of sand," said Karen.

"So was her bottom," Kathleen said.

"Mommy was crying, 'My baby, my baby,'" Karen added.

They rocked a little faster. "My baby, my baby," they cried a little more softly in their singsong voices. The twins were the child stars of their own story.

"Earplugs, anyone?" Grace said, and turned back to the book.

Mark hung around the edges of this event, his role undefined. He must have talked Mother into letting him bring glasses of lemonade to the porch for Grace and me so that he could seem grownup.

Every time I drifted off to sleep, a horrible image waited for me: me, a hairless wet dog on the beach; me, a bug in a peanut-butter jar full of water.

"Here's dinner," Mother said, setting up a TV tray decorated with little butterflies that I had never seen before. "Ice cream cones for dessert."

Dad followed with an identical tray for Grace; like my tray, Grace's bore a plate with a hot dog, potato salad, and canned peas. "Royal treatment for today's royalty," Dad said.

"Grace, would you like to stay overnight with Margaret?" Mother asked.

She must have been really rattled about the lake incident. Mother hated sleepovers. Girls stayed up too late, she be-

lieved, and talked about letters they read in Dear Abby, and got silly about boys.

"Sure," Grace said, straightening up in the lawn chair. "I'll tell my mom that I'm needed here."

We watched *Gunsmoke* with the rest of the family except the twins, who, for Mother's sake, were put to bed at eight o'clock every night. Then Mother got a pair of my pajamas for Grace. Before we went to sleep on the porch, we talked a little, but I was too tired to stay up late. I was just glad to have Grace with me.

"I'll call you later," Grace said in the morning as she left to get her bike out of our garage. "Stay dry."

"We're leaving for church," Mother said soon after, standing in the doorway in her powder blue hat, a half shell on her head. Her cheeks were rouged, and she wore a blue-and-white print dress and white high heels. Her clip-on earrings were flowers with rhinestone centers.

Grace had joked that mothers could pass as human being on Sunday mornings and when they went to weddings. "Otherwise, never let them out of the backyard," she said. "Th can mix with their own kind there."

After everyone left the house and I heard the station wag pull out of the garage, I fell asleep again. I woke up wit start. Sherman and Mr. Underwood were staring at me throu the porch door.

"You have visitors, Margaret," said Mr. Underwood. "Y

I wasn't remarkable. I was angry and sad. I wanted Sherman to disappear.

"We'll be off now," said Mr. Underwood. "We all have a lot to ponder."

Mr. Underwood knew how to be a grownup without being a stupid one. All the help in the world might never be enough for Sherman.

The Fourth of July promised to bore me. The cousins we normally celebrated holidays with were at a lake cabin for the week. That left us alone.

"We'll have a picnic in the backyard," Mother said. "We'll have a wonderful time by ourselves."

Every once in a while—and with the help of photo albums—I remembered life before the other kids arrived. Mother and I had picnics, just the two of us. We went to the park every spring and summer and fall afternoon that didn't have a downpour, even after Mark was born. I think I liked her then.

Today a picnic meant that we would carry buns and watermelon out the back door, which was easier than packing up the car and stuffing the kids inside to meet our cousins at the right time. Mother got a little break this year.

"Be careful with the burgers, Hal," she instructed Dad. He didn't take pride in grilling as did some dads, who wore aprons that said "I spear it. I cook it." But he did like to talk while he stood around and shoveled patties onto the grill.

"Mel, over here," he called to Sherman's dad. Sherman's family didn't seem to understand holidays. Sometimes, on a warm Easter Sunday, the kids would be outside eating popcorn out of a grocery bag when it was actually time to have a ham dinner. Or they might drive off to a movie on Thanksgiving just when other people were putting the pies on the table.

Sherman's dad smiled across the fence. "I'm on my way, Hal," he said. "Don't suppose you have a cold one for me?"

Dad produced a cold one from the aluminum cooler. He brought it out for picnics, even backyard ones, filled with ice and a few lonely beers.

We always begged for pop. "I'm not going to spend grocery money on Coca-Cola when we can make our own drinks," Mother always responded. We made Kool-Aid, or lemonade from lemons.

Sherman's dad sat down in the middle of the picnic bench, his back leaning on the table. He smiled at his cold one before he took a gulp. "This is the life," he said.

Next door Mrs. Jenson shook a sheet over their picnic table as if she were trying to put out a fire. She and Mother had stumbled on the idea that it was cheaper to use a sheet than a tablecloth, and no one would know the difference. Except for anyone who had ever slept in a bed.

"Mel, why don't you drag your table over here?" Dad asked, pleased with this neighborly plan.

"That's not a bad idea, Hal," said Sherman's dad. "The more the merrier."

This is brilliant, I thought, my stomach cramping in distress.

Sherman's dad put his cold one down on the table while he stood up and yelled across the fence, "Honey, get the boys to bring the table over here. We've invited ourselves."

Mrs. Jenson's expression was colder than the cold ones. The Jensons might eat popcorn on Easter, but they didn't break into other people's holidays. "I don't know about that," she said. "We have a picnic right here."

"Send it over," said Sherman's dad. "Let's celebrate together."

"What about Ruth?" she inquired. "Does she know we're coming?"

"Ruth!" Dad yelled to Mother, who was inside the house. "The Jensons are joining us, all right?"

Mother stepped outside and gave Dad a look. Men, it said. Why do they mix up food in the backyard when they don't even make it? Then she walked over to the fence. "It's fine, Joan," she said. "Bring the boys. I'll just grab a few more paper plates."

"No, no," said Mrs. Jenson. "We have our own plates. Sherman and Bobby are the only ones home. Gary went driving.

"Sherman!" she screeched to her back porch. "Bring the picnic table next door."

Mrs. Jenson began marching her food over. She brought

pigs in blankets, an exotic offering in our yard. She carried a bag of doughnut holes and a bag of jelly beans, and a fruit salad with more miniature marshmallows than fruit in it. Her third and fourth trips were eyepoppers: a relish tray of celery filled with Cheez Whiz, a pan of Rice Krispies Treats, and bottles of Orange Crush. Mother brought out her potato salad, and grapes and wedges of watermelon for dessert.

Sherman and Bobby each picked up an end of the Jensons' picnic table. It moved out of their backyard and out of sight momentarily on its journey across the front of our house and into our backyard.

"You're tearing up the lawn," yelled Mr. Jenson to Bobby, whose side of the table dragged. Mr. Jenson was very considerate, especially since he didn't value the grass on his own property. He jumped up and helped Bobby. Then the Jensons set the table next to ours, making one long table. Sherman didn't look at me.

"Aren't these kids the same age?" Mr. Jenson asked Dad, taking Sherman and me in with a sweep of his eyes. "Why don't they ever talk anymore?"

Sherman looked stricken. He dropped to a crouch next to the table leg, his fingers lightly resting and toes ready to spring. At the starting line of an imaginary race, he stared straight ahead.

"And he's off!" called Mark as he came out the back door.

Everyone stopped to watch Sherman, who lifted his backside a little higher. Then he peeled away, high-tops skimming the grass. He kept going until he rounded the front of our house. From the sandbox, the twins screamed and clapped their chubby palms. Sherman's bad comedy act was a cover-up. He hadn't figured out a comfortable way to be near me yet.

"You've got a character there, Mel," said Dad.

"He's a character, all right," said Mr. Jenson, smiling.

Mrs. Jenson looked pained. We knew that she would rather have one girl than three characters in her family.

When the burgers were done, Mrs. Jenson yelled over the fence for Sherman to come back and eat. He and Bobby sat at the far end of the table with Mark. The adults sat in the middle, and the twins and I sat at the other end. I thought of how much fun we always had at the lake with our cousins. Now I had to work hard to avoid looking at Sherman.

"Margaret, the caterpillars like it when we peel the grapes," said Kathleen.

"Then they eat them," Karen said.

"Peel our grapes, peel our grapes," Kathleen repeated in a squeaky voice. Karen joined her. They only needed one head between them.

While I was eating my second pig in a blanket, the twins spotted Mr. Underwood two lawns away.

"Mis-ter Un-der-wood, Mis-ter Un-der-wood," they chanted. He turned toward us, hose in hand. "The little tornadoes," he boomed across the yard in between us. "A very happy Independence Day to you and yours!"

"Underwood, come on over for something cool," hollered Mr. Jenson.

"Let me give these beauties a little more refreshment," he answered, "and I'll join you promptly."

"Don't dress up," Mark yelled. "We're going to have relay races pretty soon."

Wonderful idea, I thought. Count me out.

"I'll don my apparel reserved for competitions," Mr. Underwood called back.

"Re-lay races, re-lay races," screamed the twins as they sped to the sandbox.

If anyone looked more stricken about relay races than me, it was Mother. "I'll just put the food away," she said.

Mark glared at her. He had studied with the master.

"Well, I never was good at sports," Mother said. "I never even learned to ride a bike."

"It's just for kicks," Dad said. "Probably none of us can compete with Charles here, anyway." Mr. Underwood laughed his hearty laugh as if Dad had said something really funny.

"I can hold my own with a golf club, but I wouldn't presume to engage in serious competition with any of the athletic youth on the premises," he said.

Mother and Mrs. Jenson bustled around putting everything away except for the watermelon and desserts. Then we moved the picnic tables over to one side of the yard. Mark put himself in charge of races. First he went into the house and returned with two pitchers filled with water and two jelly glasses. Then he told us to form two teams, men and women. We didn't trust the twins to go in the right direction, so Karen was assigned to Mother, and Kathleen to me. I would run alone, too, as would Mrs. Jenson. Mr. Underwood volunteered to be the fifth runner on our side.

"I choose to be in the midst of a beautiful garden," he said.

"Where do children go?" Karen asked.

Mother said, "With their mommy."

Karen smiled slowly, as if she had been singled out for recognition.

"What you do," said Mark, who had placed a pitcher and a glass on each of two side-by-side lawn chairs at the back fence, "is run to the pitcher and fill up the glass. Then you run back and tag the next person, who runs to the glass and drinks the water. That person runs back and tags the next person, and that person runs up and fills the glass again. Like that, till one team finishes the water." He paused for breath, as if he had just done all that running.

Kathleen and Karen took off for the back fence. Mark tackled both of them and pulled them back to the starting line, a clothesline pole. Mother leaned down and explained the game to them, as simply as possible, with a lot of gestures. The twins didn't speak. They were aliens, transmitting their own rules to each other through their eyeballs.

"Do you understand?" Mother said.

"We want to *share* the water," Kathleen said. It was the first time I had heard either one of them use that word.

"Karen, you'll go with me," Mother said, "and Kathleen, you're with Margaret."

Because the twins were unpredictable, the women were granted a head start of ten seconds.

Mrs. Jenson started off against Mark. She ran standing straight with her arms stiff at her sides. When she reached the water, she turned around and said, "We shouldn't be drinking out of the same glass." Then we waited for her to walk briskly to her house for paper cups while the twins raced back and forth until she returned.

Even with the ten-second head start, the women's team seemed doomed when Sherman ran against Mother and Karen. But Bobby started laughing when he drank the water, and it squirted out of his nose. The men never had a chance after that. Mr. Underwood, the last in our lineup, raised his arms in victory as he crossed the finish line.

"That was fun," Mother said. "Let's all have some watermelon now."

"Wait, wait!" Mark yelled. "We're having more races. The three-legged one is next."

"I cannot play another game," Mrs. Jenson declared. "My bunion is killing me."

Mark pulled a little tablet out of his pocket. Quickly he tore a couple of pieces of paper into strips and wrote all of our names (except Mrs. Jenson's) on them, ten in all. I wondered how he would have adapted the race if Mrs. Jenson's bunion hadn't crippled her so she had to drop out. Mark made a bowl with his hands.

"Margaret, you pick the pairs," he said.

The first two names I chose were Sherman and Margaret. "Sherman and Karen are a team," I announced. When Karen's name appeared on a slip of paper, I substituted mine. So I was paired with Mr. Jenson. Mother and Mr. Underwood would go together, and Mark and Bobby. Dad and Kathleen rounded out the pairs.

Mother went into the house and returned with her ragbag. We all tied one of our legs to one of our partner's legs. Most of the ties were strips of patched sheets. Below Mr. Jenson's Bermuda shorts, his leg hair felt creepy. I seriously questioned my decision to distance my leg from Sherman's. I couldn't imagine what Karen was jabbering about to him.

Mark inspected everyone's third leg. Bobby had to go with him because they were joined by a few strips of Dad's old red-and-white-striped pajama bottoms. When Mark determined that everyone was tied together adequately, he lined us up at the back fence. "On the count of three, pairs head for the fence at the front and then turn back," he said. "First team to touch the metal fence back here wins."

When Mark yelled, "Three!" Kathleen tried to run in front of Dad because she wanted to be next to Karen and Sherman.

Dad tripped over Kathleen and fell flat. Mother and Mr. Underwood laughed so hard that they didn't even leave the starting line for a few seconds.

Mr. Jenson and I had agreed to treat our third leg with respect and not get ahead of it. I wanted to come in first so that I could escape from his hairy leg as quickly as possible. Mark and Bobby might be our only competition. Our team touched the far fence at the same time as Mark and Bobby. I heard Sherman and Karen hit the front fence as we turned our "leg" around and faced the second half of the race. Sherman chanted, "Step, step, step." Karen faced Sherman as she stood on his feet and let him do the stepping. She hung on for the ride.

Mark and Bobby panicked. They fell just a little ahead of us and started crawling, dragging their third leg as if it were something about to explode if they didn't get away from it. They passed Mother and Mr. Underwood going the other way. Mother and Mr. Underwood chatted as they took baby steps, probably discussing opera or whatever they talked about.

"We're almost home, Margaret," Mr. Jenson said. The thuds of heavy footsteps and the "Step, step, step," of Sherman's voice were close by.

Kathleen, a first-place loser with Dad, clapped her hands. "We're winning, we're winning!" she screamed, forgetting which half of the twins she was.

Mr. Jenson and I tied for first with Sherman and Karen,

crashing into the back fence at the same moment. Everyone clapped except for Mark and Bobby, who were still crawling bravely.

"Good work, Margaret," Mr. Jenson said as I slipped my leg out of the loosened rag.

I felt light-headed. "Right," I said. "I need water." I walked quickly through the open gate and around the house in pursuit of the hose nozzle.

"Margaret," called Sherman. "Wait."

Sherman ran after me, still attached to Karen. He had slid her up and off his feet, now supporting her weight on his upper thigh. She resembled a startled passenger whose train had run off the track.

"I need to talk to you," Sherman said.

"I need Kathleen," Karen said to no one in particular.

Sherman looked at her as if he couldn't remember how she had come to rest on his thigh. He untied the rag with one hand as he released her. Karen slipped down and disappeared as if a magnet were pulling her into the backyard.

"I'm sorry," Sherman said. "Really sorry. I would even be sorry if I didn't like you so much. But I've liked you ever since I can remember knowing you were a girl."

I looked at him, realizing that his eyes were just a little paler than a perfect blue sky. My cousins had a husky with eyes that color. Everyone said that it looked disturbing.

"I want us to go to the lake tomorrow," he continued. Then he stopped talking.

"Why?" I asked.

"Because," he said. "It's fun."

"Fun" was not a word I connected with Sherman. Longing, maybe, or anger. Even a melting feeling.

He leaned toward me. I stuck to the ground. Sherman's hands were perched on hips the way Mother's were when she was at her wits' end. Except that Sherman's hands were on *my* hips, as though he couldn't keep his balance without my support.

"Why are your hands on me?" I said in a thin, scratchy voice.

"I don't know," he said, looking puzzled. "I think because I love you." Sherman's face leaned into mine, and he kissed me on the cheek. His lips were dry. I wondered what my face felt like to him. Maybe glue? He seemed to be stuck there.

"Oh, yuck, I think I'm going to throw up," said Mark. Where had he come from?

Sherman straightened and took his lips and his hands back. He glared at Mark. "Hey, Mark," he said. "I can see into the future. Your life will be a lot shorter unless you keep what's private to yourself."

"Oh, right, Sherman," Mark taunted. "What are you going to do, spray me with your squirt gun?"

My eyes narrowed. "Don't even think about it," I said to Mark. "I have so much dirt on you that you might as well forget about seeing the sun again if you tell."

"Like what?" Mark asked, one side of his mouth turned up with assurance.

"Don't push me," I said.

Mark looked very unhappy. "Smoochy, smoochy," he said in a singsong voice to both of us. But he ran off.

"I'll meet you at the corner at one o'clock tomorrow," Sherman said. "On bikes."

He turned and headed for his front door.

From the backyard, Mr. Jenson's voice carried. "Cold ones for the winners," he shouted. "And the losers."

During the night a storm hit. Rain poured in through the screens. Mother tried to rouse me to come in from the porch, but I wouldn't wake up enough. She leaned over me and closed the combination windows.

The morning was cool, but it might have been because my sheets were a little damp from the rain. I huddled under the covers. Kathleen came out to the porch to yell at the middle of my back, which she thought was my head.

"We can't open the refrigerator because the cold will come out," she informed my spine. " 'Don't open the refrigerator,' Mommy said, 'No, no, no!' "

The refrigerator's problem was lack of electricity, but my problem was stickier. When I had woken up, Sherman's face was the first thing I saw with my eyes shut. Kathleen pulled on the covers.

"I'm coming, I'm coming," I said, knowing that she wouldn't leave until I acknowledged her trouble. She left chubby footprints on the floor. Mother must have missed shutting a window on the other side.

In the kitchen, Kathleen stood in front of the refrigerator. "Don't open it!" she screamed, as if I were flinging her out of the way.

Karen sat at the table eating dry Kix with a spoon.

Mother emerged through the basement door. "The power went out during the storm," she said, bucket in hand. She didn't look so lighthearted without Mr. Fun Underwood tied to her. "If we keep the refrigerator closed, we might save some of the perishables."

"We can't have our pare-iss-ables," Kathleen moaned, flinging her arms heavenward.

"Mrs. Jenson would probably buy her in a minute," I said to Mother.

Mother looked grim about my quip.

"Mom, phone," Mark yelled from the dining room.

Mother's lips pinched themselves together for my benefit. But in a minute she was chirping into the mouthpiece. "Oh, that's such a nice idea," she exclaimed. "I'm sure they would love to come over."

I prayed that I wasn't part of the "they."

Mother was more relaxed when she returned to the kitchen. "Mrs. Underwood wants you to bring the twins over for lunch," she said. "They tried to pack all their food from the refrigerator into a cooler, but she said they would like to eat up what won't fit."

"Lunch?" I wailed. "I haven't even had breakfast. Maybe I have plans, anyway."

"It looks to me as if you had plans to sleep all day," said Mother. "It's almost eleven-thirty."

"Mommy, my shoes, my shoes!" Kathleen screamed. "I need my shoes."

Karen stopped eating her cereal, stunned by her good fortune. The twins didn't get out much.

"This might be the first and last time they're ever invited anywhere in their lives," I said. "Does Mrs. Underwood know they make peanut-butter-and-Kleenex sandwiches when they're not watched? Will she enjoy seeing them lick the salt-shaker?"

Mother looked crestfallen. She knew they weren't my twins. I didn't have to take them. But maybe she had glimpsed an hour alone: a gift of time to use to scrub the porch floor without twin feet on it, or a few minutes to sit on the porch with a sandwich of her own instead of eating their crusts.

"I have plans," I said. Hadn't she forfeited her right to plans by having children?

"It's for lunch," said Mother. "Just for lunch, not the whole day."

"Put your clothes on, Margaret," screamed Kathleen. "Hurry, hurry, hurry!"

Mrs. Underwood met us at her front door. "You little dears," she said. "I'm so happy to see you. I've been up since before dawn, knowing that the power was out. I was determined to make something pleasant out of the inconvenience. And here you are!"

I couldn't look away from Mrs. Underwood's eyebrows. She had four of them. Her lower, natural eyebrows were mostly gray. About a quarter-inch above each of them was a reddish-brown penciled-on eyebrow. The twins, busy examining the contents of the candy dishes, hadn't noticed.

"Come along," Mrs. Underwood said, all of her eyebrows raised. "We have lunch waiting for you in the dining room."

Mr. Underwood entered from the kitchen. "Mother, Mother, still so vain," he said with a wink to me. "You should never put on your eyebrows without a functioning lightbulb in attendance."

Mrs. Underwood left the room smiling. She would be a lot easier to talk to without the extra eyebrows.

"I had to attend to the effects of last night's rage," Mr. Underwood said with his nothing-can-stop-me smile. He presented the dining room table with a vase of yellow roses that were only a bit battered.

Mrs. Underwood's chicken salad sandwiches were cut into triangles and speared with colored toothpicks. Radish roses floated in a glass bowl. The red Jell-O was in slightly melting cookie-cutter shapes: hearts and diamonds. This must be yesterday's labor. She couldn't have molded Jell-O without refrigeration.

"Another sandwich, Margaret?" Mr. Underwood offered.

Did he and his mother usually eat Jell-O shapes for lunch? The Underwoods were a little hard to understand. A plate of petits fours waited on the buffet. I recognized them from the picture in *Betty Crocker's Picture Cook Book*.

The twins ate as if they had been starved for a long time, stuffing sandwiches and Jell-O hearts into their mouths. I wanted to eat more, but my stomach told me that it was a bad idea. The churning inside me grew with each minute that ticked by on the Underwoods' grandfather clock in the living room. The last chime must have been at twelve-thirty. The Underwoods carried the conversation while my stomach knotted.

"Wouldn't it be wonderful if the girls could stay for the afternoon?" Mrs. Underwood said. "You could get some of your toys from the attic, Charles."

"Mother, I do believe that the few diversions I had as a child have turned to dust," said Mr. Underwood.

"Oh, nonsense," Mrs. Underwood said. "I'm sure that the girls would like to see whatever you can find."

"We should ask Margaret whether she plans to grace us with her company after lunch," he said. "If I'm to be in charge of the entertainment, I would be delighted to teach them how to play croquet. Or tennis at the park. Margaret and I would bring two capable ball retrievers."

"Well, I'm sure the girls would be very good at anything," Mrs. Underwood said, beaming at the twins, who were seated next to each other. Kathleen's upper lip, colored by cherry

Jell-O, extended in the direction of her nose. Karen's face was hidden as she licked melted Jell-O from her plate.

"I have to leave, but I know they would like to stay for a little while," I blurted out. "I'll go tell my mom that she can pick them up later for their naps." I backed out of the dining room, hoping that no one would stop me.

"Thanks for the nice time," I said. "Very nice. You girls be good."

The twins looked surprised that anyone would ever leave such a desirable place with dessert still to come.

"Bye," Kathleen said. "See you tomorrow."

"We'll come home tomorrow," said Karen, Jell-O juice dripping down her chin.

"Mrs. Underwood will tell you when that is," I answered, feeling as though I might miss today if I didn't hurry.

After escaping, I ran home and around the side of the house to the garage. Then, with my bike leaning against the back steps, I opened the back door and yelled, "I'm going on a bike ride. The Underwoods want the twins to stay until nap time. Somebody has to pick them up."

"Mom's in the basement," Mark hollered from deep inside the house.

"Tell her what I said," I called back. "All of it. Now."

I pushed my bike through the front gate, not bothering to shut it, since the twins weren't there. Then I rode down the lawn, over the curb, and toward the corner where Sherman would be.

He waited, holding an old metal lunchbox in his hand.

I didn't know what to say. "Hi" seemed too familiar.

"What's in there?" I asked, pointing at the lunchbox, which had several holes pounded in the top. "It's making noise."

Sherman held it at eye level and peered in. "You'll have to

find out when we get to the lake," he said. Hanging the lunchbox over his handlebars, Sherman seated himself on his bike. The lunchbox scratched its insides.

The day was another baker. Biking created a breeze, as long as we didn't stop. We skirted the cemetery, then the bird refuge that stretched along the curving ribbon of sidewalk to the lake. Almost every kid in the neighborhood had been in the bird refuge with its hard-packed dirt paths and dense little forest that barred sunlight from entering.

In the summer rumors crept out: a nylon stocking or a necklace had been found; thudding noises reached the ears of a paperboy early in the morning; a hand reached out and grabbed the foot of a kid foolish enough to go in alone.

Grace went in once with her dad and the little kids in her family. "There's nothing to do but walk around a bunch of old trees in old mud," she had reported. "Unless you like hundreds of birds using your head for a toilet."

Although I had laughed, I knew I would never go into the bird refuge alone until all the trees had decayed into wood chips.

Sherman braked as soon as we reached the lake.

"What about the beach?" I asked, even though I wasn't wearing my bathing suit.

"You have to see this," he said.

My bike and I followed him down to the shore where swimming was not allowed. He unclasped the catch on the lunchbox and flipped the top open. The tiny head of a baby squirrel peered over the edge. Sherman scooped the squirrel up and put it down next to his feet.

"Watch," he said. "You won't believe it." He walked in the grass and weeds that grew up in the sand. The squirrel followed Sherman, never taking its eyes off his high-tops. When Sherman stopped, the squirrel tried to run up his leg. The incline was too steep. The squirrel only got to the top of Sherman's shoe, and then it flipped backward. Sherman picked up the pocket-size creature and put it on his shoulder.

"Where did you get it?" I asked.

"It must have fallen out of the tree in the backyard," he said. "I think once they're out of the nest and start to smell like hot dogs or whatever's on the ground, their mom doesn't want them anymore. Anyway, it started following me around a few days ago."

The squirrel was cute, in the same creepy way that a dressed-up mouse in a book can be cute.

As far as Sherman's squirrel knew, Sherman was its mom, dad, and entire family. It wouldn't let Sherman out of its sight. I covered the squirrel with my beach towel—still sandy in my bike basket—while Sherman hid behind a tree. The little thing almost lost its mind looking for him. Then we invented games for it, placing it in Sherman's palm and watching it run up Sherman's arm to his shoulder and down the other arm.

We had so much fun that I almost forgot it was Sherman I was having fun with. If Grace had been there, I could have shared my insight: when there was a distraction, being with

Sherman or probably any boy could be okay. No wonder my parents wanted kids. They never had time to talk to each other. I was beginning to think that even having twins might be better than having to make conversation over the beef stew with gristle in it.

"What's its name?" I asked Sherman. "It has to have a name."

"*Her* name," Sherman said. "Of course she has a name."

"What, then?"

"Little Margaret," he said. "Her name is Little Margaret because she likes me so much."

Sherman stood up and ran in circles around the thick oak tree whose roots popped through the sand. The squirrel scampered after his heels. "Give me some room, Margaret," he called to the squirrel. "Margaret, just a few seconds by myself. We can't go on like this."

As he ran, he looked over his shoulder and directed his words at the low-to-the-ground Little Margaret. She looked as if she were attached to his feet by an invisible string. Was Sherman insulting me? I couldn't be sure. I didn't want to care. He was too funny.

"Please, Little Margaret," Sherman pleaded. "Let me breathe."

After Sherman ran around the tree so many times that I felt dizzy, he dropped to the grass. The squirrel was running so fast that she ran up and over his chest and then turned and came back. Sherman picked her up and looked at her twitching face. "Little Margaret," he said, "I'm going to have to talk to your mother about us. I don't know if you've had a rabies shot."

Suddenly he looked at me, pretending to be surprised that I was still there. "And who are you?" he asked. "Did Little Margaret invite you to come along?"

"No, she didn't," I said. "But somebody has to keep an eye on the two of you. Let's go. Little Margaret has to get home." I knew which Margaret had better not be gone from home too long, but it was easy to blame Little Margaret.

Sherman put her in the lunchbox and slid it onto his handlebars. On our way back, he said that he had to mow the lawn before his dad got home. "Sometimes I think they just had us so they would have servants," he said, meaning his parents. "Or they just kept thinking they would have a girl, but they didn't."

"If they just wanted servants," I said, "a couple of kids probably would have been enough. It's not as if you don't have a washing machine or something."

"Maybe it's the girl thing, then," Sherman said. "They're just lucky they didn't have twins like you did." Even though I hadn't had twins, I knew what he meant.

"My mom didn't know she was having twins until she had them," I said, trying not to get stuck on how alarming it would be if each of the boys in the Jenson family had a double.

"My mom was afraid she would have twins," Sherman said. "They're on both sides of the family. Her brothers are twins, but they were born in different years, so my grandma always made two birthday cakes, one for each birthday."

"Are you sure they were twins?" I asked. Maybe Sherman had ideas that were just a little wrong, the same way that his spelling missed the mark.

"Uncle Al was born on New Year's Eve," he said. "Grandma thought she was all done, and then Uncle Augie flew out a few minutes later on New Year's Day."

We biked around the corner onto our street. As we neared our houses, we saw Mr. Underwood walking very quickly in that direction.

"Mr. Underwood, we have something to show you," called Sherman to Mr. Underwood's back. He tapped the lunchbox and winked at me. I smiled back. I couldn't wink although I had practiced in the mirror a lot.

Mr. Underwood turned and looked at us. He didn't seem to be himself because he wasn't smiling, although he still looked very pleasant. "I'm afraid I'll have to postpone that experience for the time being," he said. "Young Mark just ran over to alert me that Miss Kathleen is missing from your backyard. I'm certain that your help will be greatly appreciated."

My mind flew backward. After the twins had returned from the Underwoods' and taken their fake naps, Mother might have let them go out to play in the sandbox by themselves.

Normally, they couldn't leave the yard because they couldn't undo the gate latches, which were on the outside. But I hadn't shut the gate that led to the front yard when I left. I was in a hurry.

"Let's get our assignments," Mr. Underwood said as he stopped in front of our house. "All hands on deck."

Mother's face was white. The two spots of rouge that she rubbed into her cheeks every afternoon before Dad came home looked like clown makeup. Mark stood next to her. She clutched Karen by the arm and stared at Mr. Underwood as he walked up the steps.

"How long has she been gone?" I asked.

"Maybe fifteen minutes," Mother said in a quivery voice.

"Holy cow," said Sherman. "She could be in Iowa by now."

Was Sherman's knowledge of geography that limited or was he trying to be lighthearted?

"We'll find the little tyke before she even knows that she's missing," said Mr. Underwood heartily. "I believe that we have enough of a posse to fan out in pairs to rein the little adventurer in and bring her home." As he was talking, Mrs. Jenson, Bobby, and Sherman's older brother, Gary, walked across our front yard.

"We had better start looking now," Mother said in a high-pitched voice with tears rolling behind it. She hadn't said anything to me about being with Sherman, a sure sign that she was scared out of her wits.

"I suggest that you boys begin in the alley and proceed north for approximately three blocks before returning on Barrett," Mr. Underwood said to Gary and Bobby Jenson.

Gary looked uncomfortable. "I guess I should know," he said to Mr. Underwood, "but what does she look like?"

As if things weren't bad enough, Mrs. Jenson yelled, "Oh, for crying out loud, Gary, it's your next-door neighbor."

Gary started to say something when Karen blurted out, "She looks just like me."

Mr. Underwood clapped his hands together and called out, "Bravo! A carbon copy, if I'm not mistaken."

He continued to issue assignments, making me wonder how anyone could be so prepared on demand. "Mrs. Jenson, you will accompany Kathleen's mother and proceed west down Fifteenth Street to the cemetery and circle back on Sixteenth," Mr. Underwood said, sparing Mrs. Jenson the company of her sons. "When any of you return to the starting point, make a circle that's wider by one street or alley. Do not hesitate to call out to Miss Kathleen, who will be hoping to hear her name resonating nearby.

"The party that finds the young lady will wait with her on these steps until we have all returned," he continued. "I have every confidence that she will be located after a minimal expenditure of energy."

The pairs started off. Mark stayed on the front steps with orders to hold on to Kathleen if she showed up. Roger Colby, who lived down the street, and his cousin from Cincinnati came to help. The elderly McCarthy sisters, Flora and Dora, walked across the street to see what was going on. Mr. Underwood had them take Karen to their duplex.

In a way, the teams reminded me of the relay races except that now my stomach was cramping for a different reason. Part of me hated Kathleen for being so stupid and leaving, and part of me wanted to find her, pick her up, and never put her down again.

Except for Mark, Sherman and I were the only ones left with Mr. Underwood.

"Where do we go?" I asked Mr. Underwood.

"Comb every nook and cranny of the park," Mr. Underwood said. "I believe that the two of you are the most highly qualified team for that assignment. As for myself, I will follow you and notify the park police that a little girl has possibly left her block."

Sherman and I took off on our bikes.

"We should split up," I said when we arrived at the edge of the park. "Let's cut it down the middle. I'll go left." Was I Grace? I had given a command. Sherman accepted this.

"Okay, I'll meet you by the thirteen bumps," he said, indicating the far end of the park. The night in the park with Sherman seemed a long time ago. But the park, as it had been that night in the dark, was strange.

Everywhere people did normal things. Two girls in short shorts smacked a tennis ball back and forth as if it were the only thing that mattered in the world. A boy about my size sat on top of the slide and stomped on a little boy's hands when he tried to climb up. A small girl, the lightweight on the teeter-totter, screamed down at the larger girl who kept her suspended. A mother with a buggy under an elm tree gently lifted the baby out as if he were the savior of the world.

These people had their regular lives. I didn't. My dumb sister had walked away. Even though her own feet had carried her out of the yard, I knew that everyone would say it was my fault.

Halfway to the thirteen bumps, I looked behind the hedges that separated the park from the busy street. Kathleen wasn't behind the hedges or in a tree or under a picnic table. She wasn't trying to reach the water fountain whose spray shot up past your mouth when you pressed the foot pedal.

But Grace was. "What are you doing here?" she asked, as I walked my bike up to the fountain.

"Looking for Kathleen," I said, feeling that Grace was the second person on my list of people I wanted to see more than anyone in the world.

"I know that," she said. "When I called for you, Mark told me she had flown the coop. I'm on my way to your house. Would the little shrimp cross the street by herself to get here?"

"Let's think," I said, hoping that Grace could help me think clearly. We sat on the curb by the water fountain. I tried to picture Kathleen's idea of freedom.

"What would she do that she's not supposed to do?" Grace asked.

"She climbs up on a chair and eats brown sugar out of the cupboard," I said. "She opens the door and calls for squirrels to come in. Looks in women's purses for nail polish. Just regular stuff."

"But where does she like to *go*?" Grace asked. "Does she ask you to take her anyplace?"

Knees appeared in front of us.

"Hi, Vermin," Grace said. "Any luck?"

"Not a sign of her," Sherman said, moving his eyes to my face. "I told some mom types what she looks like. They wrote down your address. Let's keep moving."

"Margaret is trying to think like Kathleen," Grace told Sherman.

"I'm picturing her biting the candles on her birthday cake," I said.

"What's making all that noise?" Grace asked Sherman, pointing at the lunchbox on the handlebars.

"That's Little Margaret," he said. "She probably wants some attention."

"Let's not joke right now," I said. "My sister is getting away."

"Before you start digging in my lunchbox," Sherman said, "did anyone ask Karen where she would go?"

"Why wouldn't Mr. Underwood have thought of that?" I said, surprised that Sherman could come up with such a logical question.

"That's good," Grace said, "very good, Vermin. Where *is* Karen?"

"With the McCarthy sisters," I said. "Old people really like the twins, even one of them." I put my face in my hands and saw Mother hanging up just one set of little-girl clothes on the line. If we didn't find Kathleen, not even Mr. Underwood's neighborliness could get Mother to smile again.

Kathleen wasn't a bad girl, really, just a little demanding. Where *would* she go? What did she want to do when nobody was around to tell her not to do it?

My head snapped up. "I have an idea," I said, gripped by a picture. I stood and got on my bike.

"Should we go with you?" said Grace.

"No, it's just a guess," I said. "Why don't you finish checking the park and come back to the house when you're done?"

I biked to the corner as fast as I could. When I got there, I saw Mother and Mrs. Jenson walking up Barrett Avenue toward our house. They were obeying Mr. Underwood's rule about circling back. Mother looked strange walking without a purse, a little grocery cart, or a child. As I passed them, I pretended that they couldn't recognize me because of my speed.

"Margaret," Mother called, "where are you going?"

"I have an idea," I yelled. I biked past our house, down the side street, and up the alley so that Mother wouldn't see where I was headed.

When I got to the Underwoods' garage, I hopped off my bike and ran into their backyard. The roses looked puffy and happy. No one answered the Underwoods' doorbell. I rang again, then knocked on the screen door.

"Mrs. Underwood," I called. "It's Margaret. Are you in there?"

The door was unlocked. After making all that noise, I crept as softly as I could through the kitchen. From the dining room I took a couple of steps into the hallway so that I could look into Mrs. Underwood's bedroom. She slept on her back with her breath coming out of her mouth in little whistle noises. At least she wasn't dead. I wasn't in her house to deal with that right now.

The fan whirred in the dining room window. The living room was cool, with the shades pulled down halfway. The front door stood open; light streamed in. Mother and Mrs. Jenson walked by on their way to our house.

Kathleen, seated on the floor in the entryway, turned around to look at me. She moved carefully so that she wouldn't disturb the family of little china animals that surrounded her.

"Margaret," she said seriously, "the ladies took Karen into their house. What are their names?"

"Miss Flora and Miss Dora McCarthy," I said.

"Oh, I know those ladies," said Kathleen. "I saw them, but I was playing."

"We've been looking all over for you. Mother is going nuts."

Kathleen looked at me as if I were crazy. "I'm right here," she said. "See. Right here. Do you want to play with the little animals now? No one will find us."

Kathleen put the china animals back on the little table with the curved legs. I didn't think that the small turtle went behind the larger elephant with its trunk in the air. But Mr. Underwood would understand why I didn't want to wake his mother and have her check Kathleen's work.

"We're going home now," I said. "Everybody's been looking for you."

"I was at Mrs. Underwood's house," Kathleen said.

As we walked through the dining room toward the back door, Mrs. Underwood's whistle breathing stopped for a few seconds and then started up a bit louder.

"Be quiet," said Kathleen, finger to her lips. "She's taking her nap."

Once we were outside, I wheeled my bike around the side of the Underwoods' house. Kathleen started to run ahead of me. "Get back here," I said in my meanest voice. "Pretend we're connected by a rubber band." I wanted to make sure there was no question about who had found her.

Mother and Mrs. Jenson were at the bottom of our front steps talking to Mr. Underwood. They turned and stared as if they weren't sure I had the right twin. Then Mother did something I had never seen her do except on the Fourth of July. She ran. Her arms fluttered at her sides as if they were broken wings. When she reached Kathleen, she knelt down on the sidewalk in her daytime nylons and held her.

Mother sobbed noisily all over Kathleen. Embarrassment replaced all the sick worry in my stomach. The shoulder of Kathleen's yellow top with the orange duck on the pocket was soggy with tears as Mother clenched her. Kathleen patted the top of Mother's head and looked around at everybody. "There, there," said Kathleen to Mother.

Flora and Dora McCarthy walked across the street with Karen, each of them holding one of her squirmy hands. Chocolate ice cream hid the yellow duck's head on Karen's orange shirt.

"Karen, Karen," Kathleen yelled as if her twin had been the missing party. "You're home! We found you!"

Sherman and Grace straddled their bikes.

"I hope she's not contagious," Sherman said.

"Where was she?" Grace asked.

"I tried to think of what Kathleen would do if she could go anyplace she wanted," I said. "And then I pictured the Underwoods' living room. All those little breakable things."

"Why didn't Mr. Underwood see her there?" Grace asked.

Mark and Bobby wrestled on the lawn, each trying to gain the advantage needed to push the other down the slope.

"Mark, where was Mr. Underwood when you told him Kathleen had disappeared?" I said.

"Backyard," he yelled, his face covered by Bobby's chest. They rolled down the hill together.

"She must have gone in the front door," I said to Grace.

As Mother thanked the searchers, her eyes shone with tears. She looked a little undone with her hair squashed on top by Kathleen.

Grace, Sherman, and I sat on the steps after everyone trickled away. "It's just the four of us now," Sherman said. He walked over to his bike and took the lunchbox from the handlebars. When he opened the top, Little Margaret skittered out and climbed up on his shoulder.

"You finally found someone who appreciates you for your mind, Vermin," Grace said.

"Little Margaret follows me everywhere," he said, stroking the squirrel's head with his index finger. "She loves my mind, my sense of humor, the works."

"Does she appreciate all the dumb stuff you do, like playing dead?" Grace asked. "Or trying to drown people?"

Sherman looked startled for about an eighth of a second. "She cherishes me," he said.

"Have you been taking vocabulary lessons from Mr. Underwood this summer?" Grace asked Sherman.

"Don't insult us," Sherman said, patting Little Margaret's head.

"He wins, Margaret," Grace said to me. "He used a three-syllable word. And all this time I thought he was going to have to repeat kindergarten."

Sherman rolled his eyes and twisted his head to the side so that he looked at his shoulder with Little Margaret on it. "Nobody appreciates me except you, Margaret," he told her.

Grace was smarter than I was. At the last spelling bee in sixth grade, she won with the word "supplicatory." She sparkled in school. But she understood how the world worked, too—how to joke with kids' parents, how to get the druggist to notice us at the candy counter when our heads didn't even reach the countertop, and how to talk to Sherman.

Maybe Sherman was smarter than I realized. He didn't go to the library. Were there other kinds of smartness? Did he have them? I imagined Sherman and Mr. Underwood reading poetry in Latin in Mr. Underwood's backyard. They would ask me over, just to be nice. But I wouldn't understand the poems, so I wouldn't go back.

The Jensons' front door creaked open. Mrs. Jenson yelled at Sherman as if he were a block away. "Get in here and help me make this fan work right now," she said. The cord she held was frayed, as if it had been chewed. "How can I make dinner in this heat without the fan?" The door slammed.

"Sometimes she spends all day heating up those fish sticks," Sherman said. He pushed the bike up the hill toward his backyard, Little Margaret running back and forth on his shoulders. "We won't be like her, right?" Sherman said to his little shadow. "We'll eat potato chips in a tree house when we feel like it. We'll eat ice cream out of the carton. For dessert, we'll go to the library and chew on your favorite books."

"Vermin, you wouldn't know a library if you were buried in one," Grace called, turning her head so that her ponytail flew from one side to the other. "And try to keep Little Margaret alive for a whole day. She's all you have."

Sherman turned to narrow his eyes at us. "We could live on love," he said.

Grace groaned. My face grew hot. I felt sunburned from the inside out.

Our front door opened as Sherman disappeared into his yard. Karen poked her head out. "Margaret, Margaret," she called. "Mommy is making Kool-Aid. It's red. She's singing."

Grace looked at me, her nose freckles standing out as if they were pasted-on decorations. I felt pale next to her. "We're so lucky," she said. "We have the last good brains they handed out this century."

"I know. But think about this. Little Margaret has a little brain. The twins have undeveloped brains. Mrs. Jenson has a mouth where her brain is supposed to be. The thing that saves them is that they don't realize what they don't have."

"Yup," said Grace. "We are the chosen. It's a burden to be a gift to the world. But we do our best." She lay down on the lawn with her hands behind her head. Then she blew a pink bubble that stretched so thin I could see the trees through it.

15

After the ten o'clock news, Mother put her mending away, and I slipped into the living room to watch *The Tonight Show*. I pulled a chair in front of the television so I wouldn't see her pack her thimble and spools of thread into the wicker sewing basket. The room was full of things she wasn't saying to me.

"Good night, Margaret," she said.

"Night," I said, without looking at her. She disapproved of *The Tonight Show*. It was in a class with movie magazines and sunbathing, pointless and possibly damaging pastimes. She departed for the distant back bedroom where Dad would be snoring in his summer pajamas.

I didn't watch the whole ninety minutes. Mark owed me a turn on the porch, and I wanted to read before falling asleep. The night radiated its own current, with crickets in chorus and a thickened texture to the air. Houses were wrapped in gauze; streetlights saved them from being swallowed by darkness. The porch was the earth's hub.

Flashlight in hand, I propped my book in front of me. Behind my head, something moved in the open window between the living room and porch. My heart thumped an alarm as I turned to look. A little face stared back. Kathleen's skin was moonlit, waxy and glowing.

"Are you going to play with Sherman tonight?" she said.

"No. I'm going to chase you back to your bed and tie you up with sheets. You can come out when you're twelve years old."

Kathleen considered this. "Mommy will cry for me," she said. "She wants me to go to the store with her. I help her pick out the blueberries."

"I'm going to tie Mommy up, too," I said.

"Karen will cry," she began.

"Stop," I said. "It's a joke. Funny."

"Why is it funny?"

"Why am I in this family?" I asked her. If I lived alone, I would stay up all night and watch old movies on television and sleep as late as I wanted. I would have real juice every day, not Kool-Aid. Grace could come over anytime.

"Somebody's looking at you," Kathleen said, staring past me and out the window.

The side of Sherman's head pressed against the screen. Was he trying to be funny? He wasn't looking at me, unless he had an eye on the side of his face. His cheek pushed through the screen's pores.

I put my mouth up to the window, next to his flattened ear.

"Not now," I said in a loud whisper. "She'll get me in so much trouble if she tells."

Guilt washed over me. Suddenly I had taken sides with Sherman. Out loud. The sensation was peculiar, the way I felt when I babysat for the Hoopers and hoped they wouldn't find me reading the sex chapter in their Christian marriage book.

Sherman turned so that his mouth and nose were squashed into the window. "I came to say good night to Miss Karen," he said.

"I'm Kathleen," Kathleen said. "Karen is my sister."

"I just wanted to make sure you know who you are," said Sherman. "Because sometimes you forget where you live."

"I live right here, you crazy," she said a little too loudly.

"Stop over and see Little Margaret sometime," Sherman said. "Good night, people." Sherman walked back to his porch, his white T-shirt bright in the dark.

"Who is Little Margaret?" Kathleen said.

When I turned to look at Kathleen, a scream escaped me. Mother stood behind her. Kathleen put her chubby arms out to be picked up. "*My* mommy," she said, putting her head on Mother's shoulder.

How can she like her that much? I thought. Mother made me wither inside. Why was she so popular with little kids? Why did the neighbors like her? Why had Dad married her? He wasn't a bad guy. Couldn't he find someone more fun?

Mother stared. She looked into the part of me that wanted Sherman to drape his arm around my shoulder when no one could see us. She looked into the part of me that hated her nylons with the snags and the way that her alarm went off at fifteen minutes past six o'clock in the morning and the way she always looked tired.

"What were you doing?" she asked me.

Being weary, that's what I was doing, being tired of trying to live my life and avoid trouble at the same time. "I wasn't doing anything," I said. "I was talking to Kathleen. I'm not bad. But that's how I feel when you try to catch me doing something wrong."

My face sunk into my pillow. I started crying for myself.

Mother didn't say anything. I heard Kathleen sucking loudly on her fingers as she did when she was tired or afraid. They walked away, Kathleen loudly slurping. The wet sound became fainter and fainter.

16

The birds were so delighted with the morning that they seemed to be screaming. The back door whooshed shut, and I knew that Dad would drive the car pool today. He headed to the garage instead of waiting to be picked up in front of the house, where he usually whistled on the curb. He worked for the government. That made him happy.

"They'll never go out of business," he was fond of saying.

The air felt as if it had been warmed in an oven all night, but it was fresh; no one had walked through it yet. But I wasn't fresh. All the summer days I had woken up with anticipation—with each day a present to be unwrapped—seemed something I would never have again. Waking up early, feeling doomed: that was Mother's effect on me.

The pillow was still damp. I turned it over and tried to get comfortable. When I couldn't, I thought of delicious choices such as walking in my pajamas to Grace's house or riding my bike to the lake and swimming during dog days.

But I knew what I had to do: walk the plank. My body resisted, but I marched into the kitchen where Mother rinsed out Dad's bowl with streaks of soft-boiled egg in it. "Let's get it over with," I said, sliding onto a chair at the table. "Tell me what a big disappointment I am."

In the next second, I wished to be anywhere in the world except that kitchen. Mother put her dishrag on the counter and sat down next to me. Tears watered her cheeks. She fumbled in her apron pocket and pulled out a handkerchief too threadbare to make it through another wash cycle. It would be useful enough to dry about one eyelash.

"I'm the disappointment," she said in a voice that bubbled with sadness. "I don't know what to do with you. I don't have a road map."

"But you kind of hate me," I said.

"Margaret, I don't hate you," she said, crying harder. "I just don't understand you. When I was your age, I was such a good girl. I was afraid of boys. I was afraid of everything. I stayed in my room and read."

"But you don't like me," I said, trying to get her to admit what the real problem was. "You're always suspicious."

"You are so smart," she gulped out. "Sometimes you scare me. I just don't want you to get hurt."

I stared at her. She looked defenseless, almost fragile. Her narrow shoulders sloped; her small hands clutched the damp handkerchief in her lap. At twelve, I looked down on the top of her head. A sense of power surged in me. "Why do you have to be like some big red light?" I said, horrified that my eyes were starting to blur with tears, too.

"Maybe sometimes we could talk about things that are going on in your life," she said, her eyeballs now concealed by the hem of her apron.

"Well, maybe we could," I said. "But I won't talk to you if you stare at me as if I'm some kind of criminal."

We were both startled by movement in the doorway. Mark stood there, his hair apparently having tried to escape from his head all night. "What's going on?" he said, blinking his sleepy eyes.

"You need a haircut," I said.

"Sounds like a funeral out here," he said, ignoring me.

"No, sweetheart," said Mother. "Margaret and I were just talking."

"Looks more like an eyeball cleaning party," he said.

He was getting a little mouthy. Maybe Mother didn't understand how to deal with him either. No wonder she kept having dumb little children, probably trying to get one she could figure out.

"Do you want a soft-boiled egg?" she asked Mark.

"I want to go back to bed," he said, looking at me. "If you won't wake me up again."

"If I want to wake you up, you'll know it," I said, glaring at his face with the sleep creases in it.

"Oh, Margaret," Mother said.

I didn't want her to cry again, so I patted her arm. "We'll talk," I said, wondering what I was saying, "about things."

"I'd like that," she said, sniffling. "You're a wonderful girl, Margaret."

"Okay," was all I could think of to say in response.

"When you were little, younger than the twins, I couldn't comb my hair in front of you," she said.

"Why not?"

"You had just learned to walk, and when you saw me combing my hair you thought we were going to the park or the store. You would get your little shoes for me to put on you." She smiled at the memory.

"I must have been brilliant," I said, secretly impressed that I had made the connection between not looking like a freak and going out in public.

"You were," she said, "and you still are."

Someone knocked at the back door, even though the bell was working again. Mother hopped up and opened the door for Mrs. Jenson.

"If I can borrow some sugar, I'm going to start on Sherman's birthday cake," she said. "I had enough at the beginning of the week, but those boys went through it for Kool-Aid when we ran out of soda."

She caught sight of me, sitting at the table in my pajamas. "What I would give to have a daughter to sit and talk to," she sighed.

"You can borrow one of ours whenever you want," I said. "They're good and sticky."

Mother looked at me, maybe wondering if I hadn't changed after our little cry.

"They even have jelly under their fingernails," I said to Mrs. Jenson.

Mrs. Jenson gave me a puzzled look. "I would love to have had the chance," she said.

Mother tapped the top of the second largest canister that sat on the countertop. "Take what you need," she said to Mrs. Jenson, who held a glass measuring cup. "And thank God for the nice boys you have."

Sherman's birthday was on Bastille Day, July fourteenth. Mother, who was a French major in college, commented on it after Mrs. Jenson brought Sherman home from the hospital. Mrs. Jenson hadn't been aware of Bastille Day. After Mother told Mrs. Jenson about the French revolution, Mrs. Jenson always made blue, white, and red frosting for Sherman's birthday cake.

"Come over for some cake after dinner," Mrs. Jenson said to Mother later in the backyard. This was a strange invitation. We ate at six o'clock. Sometimes the Jenson kids walked around outside eating pizza or a hamburger at nine or even ten o'clock at night. I didn't want to be reminded of Sherman's birthday. What were you supposed to do for someone's birthday when they loved you?

Mother always gave Dad a present, but she could be nice to him in public because they were married. "Ruth, you're the only present I want," he would say to her. Every year she gave him a can of salted mixed nuts from the drugstore. The clerk wrapped it for her.

"I especially like the cashews," he'd continue, munching as if he had a mouthful of steak. "Everybody have some." And he would pass the tin, and everyone except the twins, who could choke on nuts, dipped in. Then Dad put the nuts, along with the cards we made for him, on the mantel over the fireplace. He liked to eat a few nuts each evening until they were gone. That kind of moderation drove me crazy.

This year, July fourteenth was quiet, with a hot curtain of air waiting to fall on everybody's head if they moved too fast. In the afternoon, I offered to take Kathleen and Karen to the park so that I wouldn't have any more talks with Mother. The twins looked sweaty after their short naps.

"Let's race," said Karen to Kathleen. Heat didn't bother them. They ran ahead of me down the sidewalk. A lot of the race involved turning to look at each other. The other was always right there. Just as they were identical in looks, they seemed to have identical abilities. One couldn't pull ahead without the other being pulled along.

Moving through the heavy air, I took a piece of bubble gum out of my pocket and read the comic. Now the twins ran back at me, sure to start the race over when they touched me, the finish line. Maybe there was something worse than twins: having only one little sister. Then I would have to be in the race, not just make sure that the race didn't go out into traffic.

Sherman sat on top of the monkey bars. He was visible from the edge of the park after we crossed the street.

The twins saw him, too. "Sherman," they said, hugging each other as if having your next-door neighbor at the park was some kind of wild game.

Sherman saw us coming. He sat with his legs dangling through the bars and his arms out at his sides. As we got closer, we saw a little furry ball running back and forth across Sherman's outstretched arms.

"Little Margaret, look who's here," Sherman yelled. Little Margaret stopped and stared as if we were coming to put her in a sandwich. She scrambled into Sherman's T-shirt pocket. For a few seconds Sherman's pocket bulged and moved. Then Little Margaret's head popped up. She looked out with the confidence of someone suited in armor.

"Please, let me hold her," screamed Karen, running up to Sherman. Kathleen was neck and neck with her as they ran through the sand that slowed their progress. I dragged behind, wondering what to say. "Happy Birthday" seemed too personal when you hadn't said it since that person had stopped inviting girls to his parties.

"It's Sherman's birthday," I called to the twins. "Be nice. Don't kill his squirrel."

"Her name is Little Margaret," Sherman said, looking at the twins. "Would you like to watch her?"

Kathleen jumped in front of Karen and put her hands out,

palms up. Sherman dropped down through the monkey bars. "You'll take turns, right?" he said, taking Little Margaret out of his pocket. The girls nodded as if they were two windup toys set in motion a few seconds apart.

As soon as Sherman put Little Margaret into Kathleen's hands, the squirrel leaped out and landed in the sand. She climbed Sherman and settled on his shoulder, peering at us. Sherman gently scooped her up. This time he placed her on Karen's shoulder. Karen froze.

"Walk over to the slide," Sherman told her. He turned to look at Kathleen. "You walk behind Karen and keep an eye on Little Margaret."

They walked in a solemn procession: Karen with the squirrel on her neck, and then Kathleen. Little Margaret looked more scared than the others. As Sherman and I watched, Little Margaret tried to part Karen's hair as if it were a curtain that she could hide behind.

"Happy Birthday," I said to Sherman because I couldn't think of anything else to say.

"Right," he said, not seeming to know an appropriate response. He moved toward the teeter-totter, and I followed. When he sat down on one seat, I pulled down the one that was in the air and sat on it. I went up. Sherman bounced his feet in the sand so that we would be more balanced, although I stayed a little higher. We bounced on the teeter-totter for about a minute. Then the twins came back to us.

"She likes the slide if you hold her," Karen said. Little Margaret poked her head out of the pocket in Karen's shorts. Her eyes bugged out more than I remembered.

"You're doing a great job," Sherman told them. "Does she like the sandbox?"

The twins eyeballed each other. "Little baby, your mommies are taking you to the sandbox," Kathleen said to Karen's pocket.

"My mom said you're coming over for birthday cake," Sherman said from his seat on the teeter-totter.

"I think we are, if Mother lets us," I said. "We're a lot of people."

"She's making a couple of cakes," Sherman said. "She asked Mr. Underwood and his mom, too. She thought it was really fun when we had Fourth of July in your yard."

Just thinking about the Fourth of July made me blush. The heat crept up from my neck. Could I make Mark swear that he would never tell Mother that Sherman kissed me? I would work on it. Sherman had sounded threatening, but any threat needed to be updated.

"I guess we'll come over, then," I said. This time talking was harder than the time we were together at the lake.

The twins returned. I was relieved to see them.

"Margaret, can you push us on the swings?" Karen asked. Little Margaret had plans. She jumped off Karen's shoulder and ran in small circles under Sherman's seat.

"Here I come," Sherman told Karen as if she had asked him.

The twins couldn't sit next to each other because other kids had filled most of the rubber seats. Sherman and I pushed them two swings apart, which was perfect. Then we switched places. That way each twin had a chance to shriek about being pushed so high that Sherman could run underneath.

"Mommy, Sherman was at the park," Kathleen called to Mother, who was sweeping the front steps.

"He had his baby squirrel," Karen said, running up to Mother. "What is her name?" She turned her head to ask me.

"Little One," I said.

"No, no," Kathleen screamed. "It's Little Margaret."

Mother gripped the broom and looked at me as if I were hiding something.

"It's a joke," I said. "He thinks it's funny."

"Do you?" she asked.

"Kind of," I said.

"Did you plan to meet him at the park?"

"How would I know he was going to be at the park?" I said, my voice loud and shaky. "Do you think I have mental telepathy?" Had anything changed? After our talk, I believed that Mother might try to be a human being. Now I felt guilty, and I hadn't even planned any sneaky stuff yet.

"It's just that you're not old enough to be dating. That's all. Grace called," she continued. "She wants you to call her back."

"Okay," I answered as I headed for the front door.

"Margaret," Mother said to my back, "thank you for taking the girls. I don't know what I would do without you."

"Sure," I said. She was trying to be human.

On the phone, Grace couldn't believe that I had forgotten we were going to the library. "How could you?" she said. "It's too late now. I have to make supper. We can't be friends anymore."

"Why don't you come to Sherman's party tonight?" I asked, knowing that Grace was never upset for more than one second. "Then stay overnight at my house."

"Okay. We can go to the library tomorrow."

"Sure. Bring your books with you. I'm going to hang up and ask my mom if you can stay over. So just show up after dinner."

For dinner we had liver and bacon. I was glad I hadn't begged Grace to come for that. As soon as she arrived, she pulled the dish towel off the towel bar and started drying so that I would be done in the kitchen sooner.

Dad paused in his walk through the kitchen. He always had time for Grace because she was one of the few kids not afraid of parents. "Hey, stranger," he said. "Your old man let you have a night off for good behavior?"

"Sure did," Grace said, wiping a jelly glass. "He wanted me to come over here to teach the twins a thing or two. I heard those goofballs were drinking out of their snow globes again, so I'm going to have a little talk with them."

"Keep up the good work," Dad said. "See you at the event."

"He's funny," Grace said when Dad exited the back door. "And he never hangs around, just keeps moving." Even though Grace didn't mind parents very much, she always knew when Mother was displeased. But disapproval bounced off Grace.

"Sherman thinks that I'm his girlfriend," I said, my hands busy with the greasy frying pan. "He keeps asking me to do things with him."

"Are you?" Grace asked. "His girlfriend?"

"I'm not sure," I said. "Do we know anyone who has a boyfriend?"

"Ann O'Riley and Mike Foster went out last year," Grace said. We were dumbstruck just thinking about them. Ann's honey-colored hair swung in a perfect pageboy that brushed her shoulders. Her body curved so softly in the right places that other girls looked weird next to her. Mike was the tallest boy in the class and the best basketball player on the team.

"They stand around a lot on the corner after school," I said. "He smokes, she looks beautiful. She knows how to talk to his friends."

We went quiet again. Everyone in seventh grade knew that Ann and Mike made out in the backseat when Kathy

Springer's father drove them home from a Christmas party that Grace and I weren't invited to. That was a horrible thought: making out in a car driven by a parent.

"So they're boyfriend and girlfriend," Grace said. "But what does that really mean?"

"I don't know. I don't know if I know how to think like Ann. So how am I supposed to be the girlfriend if I don't know what girlfriends expect?"

"Ask Vermin. He's the boyfriend."

"So he has some paper with rules on it?" I said. "How does he know anything about this?"

"There you go," Grace said. "You just make it up. Nobody knows."

Kathleen and Karen appeared in the doorway. They wore matching sundresses except that Kathleen's unbuttoned buttons were in the back where they were supposed to be, and Karen's were in the front. They must have put lipstick on each other because neither one had the patience to paint her own mouth with such a heavy hand. Their lips looked swollen.

"We're going to a party," Karen said.

Mother came up behind them, and they turned to her for approval. I knew what was coming. Washcloths. Soap. Guilt.

"They're not hurting anybody," I said to Mother. In first grade I went to Diane Roome's house after school, and we made up each other's faces. I loved the way I looked that afternoon more than I ever did in my life. When I came home, Mother told me to go right to the bathroom and wash the makeup off. That's what I did. I washed my face off. I scrubbed it raw.

Mother didn't say anything as she stood behind the twins.

I knelt down in front of them. "You look so pretty," I said. "You got yourselves all fixed up, didn't you?"

They glowed. I patted their silky hair and walked into our shared bedroom, past their dresser with Mother's lipstick on it. I lay down on my bed and tried not to cry. Tears squeezed out anyway.

"It's okay, Mrs. Morris," I heard Grace say. "I used to wear my mom's lipstick all the time, and I'm kind of normal."

"Don't let her get to you," Grace said, seated at the foot of my bed. "Anyway, she didn't make them wash their little faces."

"I can't go to Sherman's," I said. "I'm a mess."

Grace brought the hand towel from the bathroom to me. One side of it was wet with cold water. "Here," she said. "My grandma does this when her soap opera makes her cry."

"Does it work?"

"No," said Grace, laughing at the thought. "We always know when somebody got sick or died."

The towel cooled the top of my face. I didn't want to get up, but if Grace went without me she would have to explain why I wasn't at the birthday celebration.

Dad, who had no idea about the lipstick and the crying, yelled from the Jensons' backyard to anyone who could hear, "The cake has arrived. There are a lot of good-looking guys out here to dance with."

"Who's there to dance with?" Grace said. "Mr. Jenson? Mr.

Underwood? Gary?" Gary was a little greasy. Comb marks showed in his hair. Dancing with him was out of the question, as if anyone would dance with all those grownups watching.

We drifted out of the house and over to the Jensons'. The picnic table was topped with a navy-blue cloth, another sheet. In the middle of the sheet stood two round cakes that displayed the French national colors. Each middle section was frosted with white seven-minute icing, flanked by blue and red. At the point at which the colors met, little peaks curled and overlapped.

The twins clapped their hands to their cheeks. They seemed to be students in a school for bad actors.

"The cakes look great, Mrs. Jenson," said Grace to Sherman's mother, who was setting the table with white paper plates and plastic forks.

"Thank you," she said, looking happy to be appreciated. "I wish my other boys had friends as nice as you girls."

"C'mon, Ma," said Gary. "Why would nice girls want to be friends with any of us?"

Mr. Underwood, his hand guiding his mother by her elbow, stepped into the yard just in time to hear Gary. "Good evening, one and all," he said in his cheerful Mr. Underwood voice. "And you, young man," he said to Gary, "should assure your mother that your words were spoken in jest. I gave my own mother some difficult times, and she has never forgiven me for the anguish I caused her, have you, Mother?"

"Oh, Charles," she said, laughing her tinkly laugh. "You

were a little dickens, but I know that you were born to tease me out of my bad moods." Silence. Were the other people trying to imagine Mr. Underwood as a little dickens or Mrs. Underwood in a bad mood?

"Mr. Underwood, you never did a bad thing in your life," said Sherman, sitting in the apple tree.

"Perhaps not in the eyes of today's somewhat more rambunctious youth," he said. "But when I invited our dog, Toby, to partake of the corned beef that Mother had prepared for a delectable St. Patrick's Day dinner, I learned that Mother and I diverged on that issue."

"You were probably just a child and didn't know any better, I'd guess," said Mrs. Jenson.

"Mother?" Mr. Underwood said.

"He was fifteen years old if he was a day," said Mrs. Underwood. "He loved that dog more than he loved the elder Mr. Underwood and myself."

"Come, come, Mother. I always knew that no matter what I did, you would be there to care for me in my declining years."

Gary looked as if he didn't know whether Mr. Underwood was kidding or not. He didn't know Mr. Underwood as well as Sherman and the rest of us did.

"Let's have some cake and not think about the trouble boys get into," said Mrs. Jenson, waving her cake knife in the air. Gary pulled a cigarette lighter out of his pocket and lit the thirteen candles.

Mr. Underwood stood and held up his paper cup of lemonade. "A toast to a fine young man on the first day of his own new year," he said. "We wish him the best of health and the best that life has to offer."

Everyone picked up his or her lemonade or cold one and raised it. Kathleen picked up her cup, and Karen followed. Their rims were ringed with lipstick prints. Dad began to sing "Happy Birthday" in his deep voice. The others joined in except for Sherman. He sat very still as though not sure what to do with himself.

When Sherman blew the candles out, Kathleen and Karen looked at the flames with such longing that Mr. Underwood suggested that they have a turn. With Sherman's help, they blew the candles out again.

Mr. Underwood and his mother settled in lawn chairs, and Mother joined them. Mr. Jenson and Dad sat at the end of the picnic table closest to the cooler with the cold ones. Mark and Bobby sat together at the other end, and Kathleen and Karen climbed into the middle section across from each other. Gary sat on the back steps near the dads after Mrs. Jenson yelled at him for trying to escape to his car with his plate. Once the little groups started talking, no one paid any attention to the twins except for Mrs. Underwood, who treated them as if they were people.

Sherman sat with Grace and me.

"So, why didn't you do anything with your own friends on your birthday, Vermin?" Grace asked, licking blue frosting off her plastic fork.

"I did," said Sherman. "We went swimming in the creek this afternoon. Smell." He tipped his head so that the top of it was in Grace's face. She took a whiff.

"Whew. I believe you, I believe you," said Grace, fanning the air in front of her nose.

"My mom hates it when I have guys over here to do stuff," Sherman said. "Big surprise."

"You know what I think?" Grace said. We didn't answer. "If your mom had all girls, she would want all boys. If she had girls and boys, she would want kids with purple eyes." She chewed slowly. "I'll bet your mom had to get married and then couldn't figure out whether or not she really wanted more kids."

The cake stuck in my throat. I couldn't look at Grace. I couldn't look at Sherman. This was not a good subject for a party. The inside of my head was empty. What could you say? With all her faults, Mother didn't wish that I had never been born. Sometimes I pretended that we were part of a science experiment, and the point was to raise a nice kid. When Mother and science were done with me and we realized that we were in the loser group, I might be nothing more than a brainless pet. But she still wouldn't complain to the neighbors about me. She would give me the good kind of dog food that makes gravy when you add water.

Sherman's pocket moved slightly. "I almost forgot," he said. "There's a show tonight. A little before midnight. I've been practicing. I mean, we've been practicing." He put his index finger in his pocket and stroked Little Margaret's head.

"My mom would kill me," I said, knowing how lucky I had been to get away with one nighttime fiasco. "I can't go."

Sherman took Little Margaret out of his pocket and held her in front of his mouth. "Please, Big Margaret, please come to my show," Sherman said in what he thought was a little squirrel voice. "Please, I'll share my berries and seeds with you."

Mother laughed at something Mrs. Underwood said. Gary burped on the steps. The dads tipped their cold ones back. I wished that Sherman would stop asking me to do things that made my stomach hurt.

20

"Why should we go outside at midnight with someone who tried to drown me?" I asked Grace. She sat cross-legged on a lawn chair on the porch. With my hands under my head, I pondered my own question in bed.

"It's so much better to *imagine* things that make you happy," I continued. "Sherman over there on his porch where I can't see him. The twins at a day camp. Me at home by myself while everyone else goes on the car trip."

"Do you have to do that again?" Grace asked, patting the place where her forehead and hair met. All the golden-red hairs tried to wind up and spring away from her head in humid weather.

"In August," I said. My parents had a twisted idea of vacations. Dad drove as fast as he could to Gettysburg or the Grand Canyon or some other place on a map. On the way we stopped at outhouses that you could almost smell from the highway. Mother heated canned chicken and the pumped water for instant mashed potatoes. When we slept at Yellowstone the summer before the twins were born, Mark and I pretended we were smoking because we could see our breath in the tent.

"What do you think Vermin has up his sleeve?" Grace asked. "We know it has something to do with Little Margaret."

"It's probably something he could do during the day," I said.

"Let's just see what it is. It can't take all night."

"I've been lucky. I never got caught for going to the park. Mark didn't tell anyone that he saw Sherman kiss me. Three strikes and all that. Why should I do something just because he asked me? Besides, does he think I take an alarm clock to bed?"

"Where are we supposed to see this stunt?" Grace asked.

"He didn't even say."

"That's Vermin," said Grace. She climbed into the double bed beside me and pulled a book from a stack on the floor. We both read on our stomachs, flashlights in hand. The crickets' racket outside sounded as if they were inviting each other to a party.

Overcome with weariness, I turned off my flashlight and stood it on the windowsill. My cheek sank into the pillow. "Good night," I said to Grace. My voice sounded far away.

"Night," she said.

• • •

In my dream, I shoved Mother into her closet. Each time that the door almost shut on her, she pushed it open a crack. My strength surged, and I neared victory, but she wedged her fingertips into the narrow space. If I put all my weight against the door, Mother's fingers—wriggling for mercy—would squish. She made a terrible noise. Her fingernails scratched on the screen next to my head.

"Margaret, wake up," Grace whispered as she tapped me on the back. "Vermin's puppet is here."

Bobby stared through the window at me. "Sherman says to come around the corner," he whispered loudly. "He's waiting."

"Let's go," said Grace. She stood in her yellow-and-white seersucker pajamas, a sleeveless top and long pajamas bottoms that her grandma had made. On Grace, they were a willow tree's wrap.

In spite of the muggy air, goosebumps popped out on my bare arms and legs. I shivered.

"Want this?" Grace asked. She held up the short-sleeved robe that matched her pajamas. My arms slid into the sleeves while my mind asked them why. Why *was* I going outside? For Sherman? For Grace? In school, free will was an endless topic. With free will, you made choices: good or bad. Some people are born without limbs. Maybe I was born without free will. Maybe my spirit was spineless, and my only choices were sneaky and sneakier.

I followed Grace outside and down the lawn toward the corner. She stopped on the sidewalk and waited for me. "Look at us," she said. "We're having a Vermin nighttime adventure together. Something to tell our dear classmates about." In a deep, slow voice she added, "If we live."

21

Is it possible to feel normal outside in pajamas? Bobby, ahead of us in his boys' shorty pajamas, never looked normal. Mother looked strange in the winter when she wore my jacket over her flannel nightgown on the way to the garbage. On the other hand, Mr. Underwood probably wrapped himself in the kind of smoking jacket that men wore in movies. He would look the opposite of how I felt.

The dark was bright.

"I'm walking through something," Grace said. "Maybe the inside of a dream."

"The inside of a dream would be filled with people doing weird things," I said.

"Maybe I'll write a book with that name," said Grace. "*The Inside of a Dream*. Or *I Walked into Sherman's Nightmare*."

We turned the corner. Bobby sat on a lawn with Mark next to him. Roger Colby was there, too, and a couple of Sherman's friends from the next block. They looked as if they were waiting for a movie to come on in the sky.

"How did you get here?" I asked Mark when I was close enough to whisper.

"Same way you did," he said, "except through the alley."

"Is this going to be worth it?" I asked.

"Doubt it," he said.

A bus rumbled by a half block away, lit up as if it were driving the sun around. I had never thought about anyone riding in a bus at night. That would be one way to avoid going home if you were in trouble.

"Where's Vermin?" Grace asked Bobby.

"He's coming, he's coming," said Bobby. "He'll be here."

"This had better be good," Grace said. "Or I want my money back." She laughed in appreciation of her own joke.

We waited. Night was a good time to wait, especially if you weren't expecting much of anything to happen. Take out the kids in pajamas on a lawn, and the night was a photograph, still on the surface, frozen with its edges bleeding on forever.

In that stillness, Sherman came gliding out of the alley across the street from us. No one even cheered when they saw him. He rode his bike onto the side street in front of us, never moving his head to look at the audience. He held a flashlight in each hand, shining the light onto his upper body. His arms moved as if they were wings, slowly dipping to one side and then the other.

"Cripes," whispered Grace. "How does he do it?"

Sherman wasn't doing much, unless you counted riding with no hands, keeping the flashlights steady, and moving his arms up and down. Little Margaret was doing all the work. She moved back and forth with Sherman's dips, from one hand and arm and shoulder to the other, always seeking the highest perch. But she didn't look frantic. Rather she seemed to be out for a run in the country, and the road was a short one on which she doubled back. Sherman and Little Margaret looked graceful together, fluid.

"I hope they're not done," Mark whispered, trembling with excitement.

We kept our eyes on Sherman as he disappeared around the corner onto Barrett Avenue. When he came into view again, the flashlights shone higher, onto his head. Little Margaret was Sherman's little hat. At first she was a blob on top of his crew cut. They rode toward us. Little Margaret fed herself with tiny fingers, dipping them into Sherman's hair.

Mark quivered next to me. "Nuts?" he said. "Seeds?"

"I'll bet you a thousand dollars," Grace said, "that it's birthday cake. She's licking stuff off her paws."

Sherman's eyes looked ahead, not at us. He made a wide turn into our alley. Was the show over? Would there be a grand finale?

He never saw the car. There weren't any lights because Gary was sneaking down the alley in his Oldsmobile. The engine's noise barely registered in our ears because Gary coasted until he was almost to the end of the alley.

Gary braked, but by that time Sherman was airborne. He flew across the side street and onto the lawn of the apartment building that I had dreamed Elizabeth Taylor lived in. Sherman bounced a couple of times, in slow motion, it seemed. His head flopped as if it were trying to shake itself off his body.

Gary popped out of his car door. "God, Sherman, what are you trying to prove?" he yelled. Then he stood there, motor running. He stuck his hand back into the car and turned the lights on his younger brother, who had stopped bouncing.

This time I didn't run to Sherman. There were no thirteen bumps to fly over. I walked across the street even though I wasn't sure what to do with my feet, which felt like concrete blocks. If I stopped, I wouldn't keep going. From behind me, I heard Grace crying, which was not a Grace-like thing to do. Bobby sniffled. The car lights shone on Sherman and into a basement apartment window, which was open a crack. A light went on inside.

Something in the middle of Sherman's forearm tried to break through the skin. When I realized that it was bone, I stopped looking there. Sherman was ghostly white, with blood at his hairline and on his forehead. I put my hand on his back but couldn't feel anything. I took my hand away and rested my cheek there and waited. It lifted a little. He was breathing.

Turning away from Sherman, I yelled in a breaking voice, "Go tell your mom and dad, you idiot."

Gary slipped into the car and backed down the alley toward his house. Grace and the other kids walked across the street toward me. They moved slowly, as if they were resisting being pushed from behind.

For a fraction of a second, I wondered if we could carry Sherman home and put him to bed. Let his mom come in screaming at him in the morning. She would finally have something to lament. Who was to blame for this accident, anyway? Sherman? His stupid brother? The audience for showing up in their pajamas, hoping the show would be worth getting caught for?

At first the scream of the ambulance was a little pinprick of sound in a hole of silence. I slipped out of Grace's robe and covered Sherman so that we kids couldn't stare at his sad, still body.

The rest of the night happened the next morning because it was after midnight. Mrs. Jenson ran down the alley, scream-ing, "Sherman, Sherman!" When she reached him, I thought that maybe she could scare him out of his unconsciousness. With a scarf tied over her pin curls, her head was the size of a grape. But she knelt down by his side and pulled Grace's robe up over his shoulders a little more. Her face had so much pain in it that I couldn't look at her.

Mother knelt down next to her. She put her arm around Mrs. Jenson and patted her as if she were one of the baby twins who wouldn't settle down to sleep. Dad and Sherman's dad stood behind the moms. They looked as if they were star-ing into a grave.

Grace's face was wet under the streetlight. When I looked at her, she snapped back into being Grace. "You almost wish they would start yelling at us," she whispered to me.

The men in the ambulance handled Sherman very gently. When they slid the stretcher under him, I couldn't bear to watch how they arranged him. Mr. and Mrs. Jenson climbed into the back of the ambulance.

"I think he's a goner," said Roger Colby.

Grace stared at him. "Sherman has nine lives, like a cat," she said.

"Or a squirrel," said Mark.

The thought was a cold wind that alerted us.

"Where's Little Margaret?" said Bobby.

Sherman had gone away mangled in an ambulance, and we were powerless. But this gave us something to do.

"Sherman will be really mad if we lose Little Margaret," Bobby said.

How do you look for a baby squirrel in the dark?

The grownups who had followed the siren now stood in a tight circle. Mr. Underwood looked very serious in his deep-red smoking jacket.

"She's probably around here looking for Sherman," said Mark.

One of Sherman's flashlights was still on, and Grace picked it up from the street. We looked for Little Margaret until Mother said, "I have to go home now. The twins are alone."

The rest of us walked down the alley in little packs. Mr. Underwood walked next to Dad, who almost looked normal. He was wearing the robe that Mark had borrowed to play a shepherd in the Christmas pageant at school, so I had seen it out of the house and onstage.

"Who knows what that bright-eyed little creature is up to," said Mr. Underwood, who slowed down so that we could catch up to him. "Was she with Sherman as he began his spectacle?"

"She was on his head," I answered.

"Perhaps she scrambled into his pocket," Mr. Underwood said. "She might be on her way to her first hospital and will share a room with Sherman as he recuperates."

Back home, Mark ran upstairs to his room as if he was sorry he had ever left it. Grace gave me a halfhearted wave and headed for the porch. Dad disappeared. I sat down on a kitchen chair. Mother sat across from me.

"Are you going to ask me what we were doing?" I said.

Mother looked tired, but not mad. "Sometimes it doesn't matter what you did," she said, "because nothing can undo it." She looked at me, not as if I were a bad kid, but as if she wanted me to listen. "If I got mad at you and Mark, would you feel worse?" she asked.

"No," I said. "I'd probably feel better because then I could be mad at you and stop thinking about Sherman."

"Well, there you go," she said. "There's nothing to do but say a prayer for him. And thank God every day that you children are safe."

Mother was so gooey that I could hardly stand it. Tears built up behind my eye dams, and I didn't know whether they were for Sherman or the sad world where mothers had to pray that their kids wouldn't be hauled off in ambulances.

"Maybe people just shouldn't have kids," I said. "It sounds like a lot of trouble."

Mother looked as if she had been slapped. "Never, ever think that," she said. "Children are the joy of my life." She paused. "And being married to your father."

"News to me," I said.

She glared at me for just a second. Then her expression softened. "You can't understand it now," she said. "You just have to believe it."

"Mr. Underwood doesn't have any kids," I said. "He seems pretty happy."

"He is," she said. "I can't speak for him. But I'll tell you something that Grandma told me when you were a baby. In front of her, I said to you, 'Margaret, no matter how many children I have, you'll always be my favorite.' And do you know what Grandma said to me?"

"No," I said. "I can't remember. I was a baby."

"She said, 'No matter how many children you have, each one will be your favorite.' "

"Nice," I said. "Very nice."

"I'm going to bed," said Mother. "We'll call the Jensons first thing in the morning."

As I walked to the porch, I wished I had asked what

Grandma would have thought about the Mrs. Jenson kind of mother.

I stopped and stood still when I heard Gary on the front steps next door. He cried as his cigarette smoke wafted into our yard. I hoped that he was upset about Sherman, not weeping about losing his car privileges or something.

Grace slept soundly. I climbed over her and let myself sink into my side of the bed by the window. I looked around the porch before shutting my eyes. It felt different. I had been away a long time.

Mrs. Jenson woke me up in the morning with her loud crying at our kitchen table. She had gone to the hospital in her nightgown, so she must have decided that it was okay to wear it in public. Her pink bathrobe looked like a flour sack from neck to ankles, so at least we couldn't see much skin. She must have seen herself in a hospital mirror because the bobby pins and the scarf that covered her head were gone. Her flattened little circles of hair hadn't been combed out, though.

"Looks like her hair went to prison," Mark said under his breath.

Sherman had a concussion, Mrs. Jenson told us, and a broken arm that required surgery. I was so glad that he wasn't dead that I touched her shoulder, although I don't think she noticed it through her robe and nightgown.

Summer didn't feel summerlike that day, but rather a day adrift, floating on shifting currents. Grace and I had planned a library trip. We decided to take the twins with us so that

Mother might stay in her gentle frame of mind. I pulled the wagon out of the garage, knowing that walking with the twins would seem to take months compared with our biking time.

"When are we at the library?" asked Karen as we started down the alley.

"When you see a lot of books that you can't read to yourself," Grace said.

"We can read," said Kathleen. "Mommy always says, 'You girls read a book and then you take your naps.' "

Karen saw Little Margaret before anyone else did. Maybe no one else would have noticed her. "Look! Look!" she screamed. "It's Little Margaret!"

The baby squirrel lay in the street pressed against the curb. Probably a detective could tell whether she had been thrown on impact or moved away from traffic by a kindhearted passerby. She was curled into herself.

"Poor baby," said Kathleen, climbing out of the wagon. "Oh, the poor baby."

I picked Little Margaret up in one of the handkerchiefs that Mother had given me. Mothers must do that: provide emergency supplies to their stand-ins. The handkerchief was perfect, something Mother couldn't have known. Embroidered with pink and yellow buds and green leaves around the border, it covered Little Margaret completely with enough extra to tuck her in snugly.

"I guess this has turned into a funeral procession," Grace

said. She pulled the wagon with the twins and our unreturned books back down the alley. I carried Little Margaret.

After we told Mother and she made us wash our hands, Grace and I went over to the Jensons'. "We found Little Margaret," I told Mrs. Jenson. "We want to bury her in your backyard, if that's okay with you."

Mrs. Jenson, now dressed and combed out, looked puzzled. "Who is Little Margaret?" she asked. Then I knew that she still had a long way to go before she'd be a mother anybody would want.

Everyone we could find came to the funeral that afternoon: me, Grace, Bobby, Mark, the twins, Roger Colby, Mother and Mrs. Jenson, and Mr. Underwood. Gary came out into his backyard for the service, looking as solemn as if he were at Sherman's funeral.

"Bobby told me all about Little Margaret," Mrs. Jenson confided in me. "When we visit Sherman today, I'm going to tell him all about this."

Mr. Underwood brought white roses and baby's breath from his garden. Only Mr. Underwood would know how those whites with wisps of green could break your heart with their beauty. Grace asked him to speak and, being Mr. Underwood, he did.

"Those of us who had the privilege of knowing Little Margaret will never forget her," he said.

Kathleen tried to break away from Mother and get to the shoe box that held Little Margaret on the picnic table. Mr.

Underwood paused to hand a rose to each twin. The rose distracted Kathleen, who buried her nose in the flower and then licked a petal, looking confused about why the flavor didn't match the scent.

"Little Margaret embodied the qualities that we strive to nurture in ourselves," Mr. Underwood continued, "curiosity, loyalty, enjoyment of the earth's beauty and bounty. I believe that were Little Margaret with us to review the events of July fourteenth, she would find mercy, not bitterness, in her heart. She died, not in the arms of her beloved, but on his head."

Mr. Underwood winked at me. "Blessed Lord, we thank you for the opportunity to have known and loved our delightful friend Little Margaret. May we find kindness toward one another to be our solace as we move forward in her memory."

Grace and I said, "Amen." Everyone else murmured it after us. Bobby and Mark placed the shoe box in the hole they had dug under the apple tree. We all took turns filling it in.

"How will she get out when she wakes up?" Karen asked Mr. Underwood when he helped her with the spade.

"She will not return to us in this lifetime," he said. "But she will live on in our hearts."

Kathleen opened her mouth with a question, but Mr. Underwood spoke first. "Would you join Mother and me for tea following the service?" he asked, including everyone in his invitation.

My first funeral lunch was more fun than I imagined the

lunches that Mother brought casseroles to at church were. Mrs. Underwood prepared "finger food." The frozen lemonade on a stick made in ice cube trays was a hit.

Later in the day, Mrs. Jenson drove off with her two non-broken sons in the station wagon to see Sherman during visiting hours at the hospital. Bobby sat next to his mother. Gary sat in the backseat that faced away from them. Mr. Jenson visited Sherman in the evening.

Time would tell. Maybe Mrs. Jenson had learned that there was something worse than having all boys. And that would be having one taken from her.

Sherman came home about a week later. Bobby spread the word. He wasn't happy because Mrs. Jenson said that Sherman could sleep on the porch by himself for the rest of the summer. But Mr. Jenson let Bobby play poker at the card table on the porch whenever he wanted.

"It's great," Bobby reported. "Mom is a doughnut factory. She deep-fries while we play poker."

Sherman's head injury made him tired. But I had to see him. "You know about Little Margaret?" I asked. Mrs. Jenson had Sherman propped up in a display of floral pillows.

"My mom told me," Sherman said. "I'm really going to miss that baby fur ball. She was kind of like the Underwoods—nice heart."

Mr. Underwood decided that reading to Sherman would help him pass the time when there weren't any good shows on TV, or when Gary and Bobby couldn't play poker because Mr. and Mrs. Jenson had decided to make them paint the house.

I wanted to choose books that Sherman might like but would never read, maybe *Tom Sawyer* or *Huckleberry Finn*. Grace voted for *The Yearling*, but I thought it was too sad for someone who might have died himself. Mr. Underwood insisted, very kindly, that we begin with one of Shakespeare's comedies, *Much Ado About Nothing*.

"We will set a high standard for our dramatic reading," he said.

When he brought his hardbound copy of the play to Sherman's porch, I flipped through it. "Oh, no," I said. "There's that Beatrice again."

When Mr. Underwood learned that my middle name was the same as that of his beloved heroine, he insisted that we take parts. Of course, he had me play Beatrice. Mr. Underwood thought that the role of Margaret, a lesser character, was beneath me. He assigned Sherman the part of Benedick, Beatrice's sparring lover.

"I can't concentrate that much yet," Sherman said. "Next play, I'll be the star."

So Mr. Underwood was Benedick to my Beatrice. Grace was Don John and a variety of other figures. Mr. Underwood assigned the other roles based on who showed up to read on any given day. Bobby hid when Mr. Underwood came over.

"After we finish the comedies, we will move into the tragedies, beginning with *Romeo and Juliet*," he said, looking as pleased as he did among his roses. Summer wouldn't last as long as Mr. Underwood hoped.

At the end of the first week of Sherman's return, I swallowed my nervousness and entered his porch before the others had arrived for dramatic reading.

"Margaret, we're alone again," said Sherman, putting down his bottle of ginger ale, which our family only offered as a warm drink when someone had a stomachache. "This is different."

I sat on a porch chair, not the one closest to Sherman, not the farthest. I trembled inside. "Sherman," I said, "if I wanted a boyfriend, you would be it. But I have so many other things to worry about."

Sherman didn't say anything. He had never really asked me to be his girlfriend, I realized. "Is it someone else?" he said. "Mr. Underwood?"

"Right," I said. "We're going to ride bikes this afternoon."

We both laughed at the picture of Mr. Underwood's legs going in circles while his proper upper half looked straight out into the world. After we stopped laughing, the porch was very quiet.

Sherman cleared his throat. "I won't do the playing-dead kind of stuff anymore," he said. He looked at me as if asking if that was enough.

I had run out of script. So I listened for Mr. Underwood's voice to get me through this. "Do whatever your heart tells you to do, Margaret," he might say. "Ultimately, we are the only judges of our actions."

I couldn't get the voice quite right, but I knew what I

wanted to do. When I leaned over Sherman all propped up in pillows, I thought I would fall on the arm cast lying at his side. But I kissed him on the cheek while I closed my eyes so that I couldn't see his face. Then I sat down in the closer chair.

He picked up my hand with his uninjured one. "Remember what I said that first night through the window?" he said.

I nodded.

"I just wanted to make sure that you heard me."

Mr. Underwood came whistling across the lawn. As he passed my house on his way to the Jensons', Kathleen yelled at him from the porch. "Mr. Underwood," she called, "do you wish I was your little girl?"

"I consider it an honor to count you among the most delightful of my acquaintances," he said, looking through the screen at her.

Kathleen ran into the house. "Karen," she cried, "Mr. Underwood wants us to live with him."

"I'm getting my babies," Karen screamed back.

Sherman's hand felt solid around mine, comfortable and new at the same time. I didn't feel quite as certain about my no-boyfriend speech. We weren't really racing through *Much Ado* with Mr. Underwood. But I thought of Beatrice's line in Act I, "I had rather hear my dog bark at a crow than a man swear he loves me." Sherman and I still had a lot of acts to get through to find out what would happen.